ON THE MANY DEATHS OF AMANDA PALMER

ON THE MANY DEATHS OF AMANDA PALMER

and the many crimes of Tobias James

edited by

ROHAN KRIWACZEK

with an Introduction to Doxithanotology from
Professor Richard D. Davenport

OVERLOOK DUCKWORTH
NEW YORK • LONDON

This edition first published in hardcover in the United States in 2010 by

Overlook Duckworth Peter Mayer Publishers, Inc.
New York & London

NEW YORK:
The Overlook Press
141 Wooster Street
New York, NY 10012
www.overlookpress.com

LONDON:
Duckworth
90-93 Cowcross Street
London EC1M 6BF
inquiries@duckworth-publishers.co.uk
www.ducknet.co.uk

Cataloging-in-Publication Data is available from the Library of Congress

Manufactured in the United States of America
FIRST EDITION
ISBN 978-1-59020-381-1 US
ISBN 978-0-71563-970-2 UK
10 9 8 7 6 5 4 3 2 1

IMPORTANT PREFACE TO THE SECOND EDITION

It may not have escaped the attention of the more diligent reader that this edition is in fact the second edition, despite being the first to make it into most bookstores. Well, as they say, therein lies something of a tale.

Around eighteen months ago, in August 2007, the first edition of this book was sent to print in a modest run of three thousand copies, although, given the extraordinary public interest in Miss Palmer's demise, it seemed certain we would be requiring further print runs in time. On August the 27th the book was launched with an extravagant fancy dress party held at Boston's Four Seasons hotel, and initial copies were shipped out to a select one hundred outlets. Pre-orders via the Amanda Palmer Trust (APT) website had already mounted up considerably, and hence we were about to order the second run. Then, quite unexpectedly, we received a visit from Inspector Ruecker and his team.

Let me be honest: "visit" is a wholly inadequate word to describe the invasion and intimidation that was to follow. All our computers were seized, both private and business; anyone working at the APT headquarters was handcuffed and bundled into the back of a police van: we spent a good twenty-four hours in and out of cells being questioned, with no real explanation as to why. Finally we were released without charge, pending further investigation, and the computers were eventually returned some four months later. All copies of the first edition were seized bar one hundred and twenty seven that had been bought for cash in bookstores and couldn't be traced. These have not been returned.

So what was going on? It seems that one of the *palmeresques* presented in the book, *Text Number Nine*, bore an extraordinary and incriminating resemblance to the circumstances of Miss

Palmer's actual death, most specifically in various details never released to the public. As is well known the investigation remains open and no one has yet been charged with the crime, nor has the nature of Miss Palmer's death ever been fully revealed, hence this text, and its connection to the APT itself, constituted major evidence, and thus was not to be published.

I must emphasize that no one connected with the APT has ever been charged, nor implicated in relation to Miss Palmer's death, however, the following investigation did uncover an extraordinary and disturbing level of corruption within the committee and in particular amongst the editors involved in the preparation and selection of materials for the book, both in the moral and political senses of the word. Needless to say, many resignations were made, and the APT now runs under entirely new management.

One of the new Board's first tasks was to address the issue of this book. Should it be reprinted with the seized text omitted? Should it be abandoned? Re-edited? However, before any particular approach could be agreed upon a new set of revelations came out with regard to the other nine texts, which resulted in one clear and more easily agreed conclusion: that the book should be reprinted as a facsimile of the original edition but with the seized text, and any other text deemed sensitive by Inspector Ruecker and his team, blacked out; additionally it should include a substantial appendix which details the true circumstances of its compilation and authorship, and the trail that ultimately led towards Tobias James.

That is the book that you now hold in your hands.

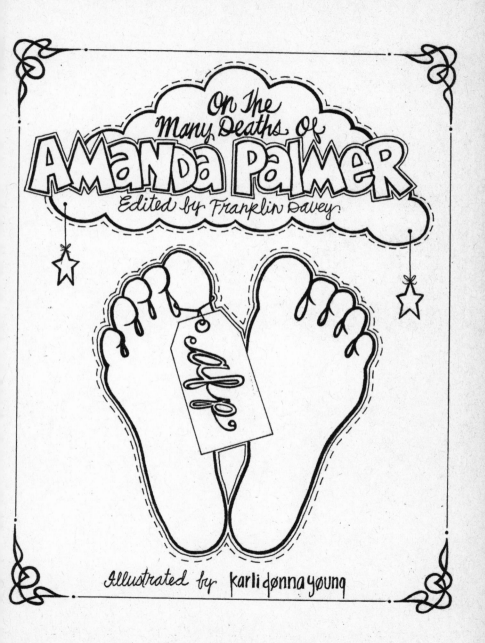

To the memory of Amanda Palmer

CONTENTS

ACKNOWLEDGEMENTS

In the course of producing this collection we are very grateful for the considerable help and assistance we have had from a great many people. It is, of course impossible to name them all, but it would be rude not to try. First we must thank our diligent team of editors who read their way through six and a half thousand texts between them in search the final ten pieces included here: ████████, ████████, ████ ████, ████████, ████████, ████████, ████████, ████████, ████████ and ████████. We are also delighted to present a series of specifically commissioned illustrations from much celebrated up-and-coming West Coast artist, Karli Young, whom, I have been assured, had met Amanda on at least one occasion. I must, of course, also thank the two eminent specialists who have contributed introductions or essays to help put this collection into context: Dr. Kyla Dufford, and Professor Richard D. Davenport, who has allowed us to include his wonderful short introduction to Doxithanotology despite the many personal issues that arose during this project. Then there were the researchers, who sought out and verified the original six and a half thousand texts: ████████, ████████, ████████, ████████, ████████, ████████, Matt Tromans, ████████ and David Francolini. And finally there are all the many friends and colleagues who in various less defined ways provided inspiration, support, and, in one case (you know who you are) "smoothies" and cup-cakes for every executive meeting: ████████, Oscar de Winter, ████████, Jonathan Walton, Schosti, Jason Webley, Linda Cleary, David and Yael Breuer, Robin Stevenson, Lance and Dawn Dann, Jared Brading (for his ceaseless optimism), John, Human, ~~Jason Dickinson~~, Rory Pierce, Max Melton, David Osmond-Smith, Guy Landver, Nik, Sara Bynoe, Clare Davies, Abigail Parry, Aoife Mannix, Matthew Gregory, Marianna Swann, Jenny Kingsley, Aviva Dautch, Edwin Morgan, Paul and Jeannette Kriwaczek, ████████, ████████, ████████, the other Richard Skinner, the other Nick Drake, Glyn Maxwell, "Sparkle Bunny", Kya Boon-Cohen, Daisy, Ben Benatt, Jo, ████████ "Flo" and so many others, too numerous to list, given that I have only been given one page . . .

It is, in all likelihood, a fair assumption that the majority of people reading this book will be well aware of the life, works and death of Amanda Palmer. But, just on the off-chance that you, dear reader, are one of an adventurous minority who have picked up this book at random, let me take a moment to briefly introduce our subject, naturally being careful not to steal the thunder of the two eminent authorities whose wonderful essays are to follow. So who was Amanda Palmer? Well, in her brief moment in the light she became many things to many folks. Her ostensible "job" was that of singer/songwriter/ performer/diva, but, like all true stars it was her charisma and infectious enthusiasm that brought her success, singing just happened to be the vehicle she stumbled upon. To her loyal fans she was more than a pop star: she was a role model, a symbol of empowerment, a doorway to another more exciting imaginative world; to her politer detractors she was "a pretty young woman who [wore] cabaret makeup and [danced] around in frou-frou knickers, suspenders and a corset singing songs about female issues"; to certain religious far right groups she was little short of the Antichrist. Her songs have been described as both "emblematic for the neo-post—Weimar-Brechtian-punk-revivalist-cabaret-pop movement of the late 1990s" and "the very worst kind of blah and pap for middle class kids to pretend rebellion to". When her almost meteoric rise was cut short under mysterious circumstances it seemed inevitable that her brief and "beautiful" life would in some way or other become iconic. However Amanda Palmer herself is not the subject of this book, nor is her death, as the title might suggest. No, the subject of this book is the extraordinary and entirely unexpected form through which her iconisation was to express itself. A form that has come to be known as the *palmeresque*.

FRANKLIN DAVEY

A BRIEF INTRODUCTION TO THE SCIENCE OF DOXITHANOTOLOGY
by Professor Richard D. Davenport

The science of Doxithanotology, that being in simple terms the study of macro-socio-psychological responses to the deaths of social icons, may not be an old science, but has, in the last few years, very much come of age. Indeed, the past decade has seen an extraordinary growth in the associated doxithanotological industries, which has in turn further excited both publishers and university departments alike. Following the unprecedented macrosocial response to the Death of Princess Diana, the study of celebrity death cults was finally legitimized as an academic discipline in September 2006 with the introduction of an MA course in Doxithanotology at the University of Bexhill-on-Sea, and many other such courses planned to follow shortly.

It is in the publishing end of the industry that this sudden surge of popular interest can most easily be observed. From worthy tomes of serious scholarly depth to cynical populist attempts to "cash in on the fad", our bookshelves have not been so weighted down with eulogies of one form or another since the early 17th century. It has even been postulated by Prof. Alasdair Remington that more Americans now own a copy of Walter McArthur's *How Did They Die?* than own a passport, and the extraordinary success of P. Jerich's *Dead American Icons* which has so far won 4 major awards including both the fiction and non-fiction categories of the Melville Prize, is entirely unprecedented. It seems we are currently a culture in the grip of an obsession with Memento Mori, and in particular post-mortem speculations of the spiritual, biographical, analytical, and conspiratorial varieties. And yet, however interesting the question of why such an obsession with memorialising has developed may be, most scholars of doxithanotology believe that the key to that answer, and indeed many others, lies not with why, but <u>who</u> we are eulogising.

It has of course been much commented upon that as a culture we are effectively canonising an ever-increasing number and variety of "celebrity" icons, but it is largely thanks to the ground-breaking work of statistician Louis le Grenier, that what had for many years been little more than a passing concern of occasional columnists was developed into a complex system of analysis capable of generating useful and enlightening data. This was not le Grenier's intention. His real interest lay with Medieval Christian martyrs. In the introduction to his ground-breaking work *A Statistical Study of Martyrdom through the Ages* le Grenier explains that as a child he had been brought up a fervent Catholic, and had read about the lives of the martyrs obsessively. When he was around 14 he began devising charts on which he plotted the dates and impacts of every martyr he knew of. Although, by his own admission, these charts were very primitive and naïve he soon began to notice certain patterns. Years later, when invited to study for a PhD in statistical analysis at the Université de Picardie Jules Verne, he decided to revisit this subject, somewhat against his professor's advice, making it the subject for his thesis. Twelve years later, and having travelled a total of almost 87,000 miles around the world in search of evidence of the impact of martyrs upon various societies, he finally handed in his 163,000 word thesis to considerable acclaim from the academic establishment. It was this thesis that was to form the initial basis of *A Statistical Study of Martyrdom through the Ages,* however, it wasn't until he met renowned Dutch popular culture philosopher Dedrick Bose that the final pieces fell into place. Until that meeting le Grenier had only concerned himself with religious martyrs. It was Bose who suggested that he should broaden his research to include secular martyrs – individuals whose deaths resulted either directly or indirectly from the determined maintenance or execution of their beliefs - and further suggested he should look at artists, scientists, and celebrity symbols of consumerism. It was only when these additional elements were factored in that the full social implications of his work became apparent.

To grasp the essence le Grenier's works, which have now become the foundation texts of Doxithanotology it is important to first understand le Grenier's four foundation precepts, as initially presented in *A Statistical Study of Martyrdom in Post-Medieval Western Civilisation*:

1. The concept of *the Transferable Vessel*: this is the long established notion that the human need for "God" is so deeply ingrained that any attempt to abandon it in the hope of escaping the vagaries of superstition merely leads to the displacement of our instinct for faith, love and absolute answers onto other symbols. Hence God was replaced by Art in the early 18th century, Art by Science in the 19th century, and Science by Celebrity Consumerism in the late 20th century. There is, of course nothing new in this thought, but le Grenier was the first to offer a formal statistical proof.

2. *The Macro-Social Martyrdom Reflex*: this more contentious theory claims to be demonstrated beyond doubt in le Grenier's paper *A Statistical Survey of Martyrdom through the Ages*, however to complete a wide ranging pan-historic test of the proof is impossible as each calculation demands the accurate knowledge of at least 224 variables calculated from details of the subject's life, death and influence, which are rarely available in practice. This problem was later addressed and a more elegant, yet still controversial, proof presented in *A Statistical Survey of Martyrdom in Post-Medieval Western Civilisation*.

Put in simple terms the theory postulates that society, and in particular the belief systems it generates, operate as a self-regulating organism. In essence this means that society requires the regular martyrdom of those who come to symbolise the spirit of their age, in order to evolve. Thus, le Grenier states, by tracing the movement of high Martyrdom Quotients across social strata and professions you can get an accurate and specific account of the spiritual aspirations and general belief systems of any given period. When an idea, or series of ideas, evolves that has the potential to dangerously destabilise the "status quo" this poisonous idea is essentially pushed out like a pimple. The mechanism by which this is achieved is the Martyrdom Reflex: amongst that strata of society infected a consensus is established by which a person or group of persons particularly enthused by the dangerous new idea come to represent it in symbolic form, thus the idea becomes contained in a mortal vessel, or icon. Often this is all that is required to undermine or limit the idea as the inherent human weaknesses of the icon will usually inspire enough disillusionment to defuse the situation. Good examples of this effect might include *Posh Spice* symbolising *Girl Power*; Gary Glitter symbolising the freedom of self expression; Bruce Willis symbolising the *New Gay*, or Tom Cruise becoming the internationally accepted symbol for Scientology. However, upon occasion, the person or persons chosen actually understand the nature of the social role thrust upon them and attempt to make use of it. This is potentially very precarious for the stability of an organised society and so society's antibodies step in (in today's Western World they would most likely be the reactionary ultra-right). Le Grenier calls these the anti-icons, and claims to have calculated that for every icon generated there are approximately 10.073^n potential anti-icons where n is the Martyrdom Coefficient for the given society at the given time. This basically means that "something's gotta give", and in the majority of cases the result is the effective sacrificing of the icon, either by their own or others' hands. In most cases, and despite an inevitable momentary increase in popular concern, this will usually have the effect of dissipating the dangerous idea through lack of a unified concerted direction and the general disillusionment that follows. Examples of this phenomena might be: the death of Marilyn Monroe resulting in the steep decline of a certain brand of smouldering female sexuality – le Grenier shows how this led to a decrease in the birth-rate of 37.6% over the following five years; the death of Jimi Hendrix resulting in the end of the naive dream of "sex and drugs and rock'n'roll", a dream whose more cynical branch finally dissolved after the deaths of Keith Moon and John Bonham nearly ten years later; the death of John Lennon which finally concluded the "we can change the world through love" movement in 1980; and in addition many more such examples may be observed over the last fifty years. As will be shown, the ever-increasing number of "mini-martyrs" over the last few decades is the direct result of the low Martyrdom Quotients involved.

3. *The Martyrdom Quotient (MQ)*: among the most important contributions of le Grenier's *A Statistical Study of Martyrdom in Post-Medieval Western Civilisation* is the development, through a series of complex and wide-ranging statistical analyses, of the now standard Martyrdom Index, by which, given the relevant data, the specific martyrdom quotient of any individual can be calculated to three decimal places on a scale of 0-27. The devising of this scale had the additional intention of demonstrating his own theory of the macro-social-martyrdom-reflex (see above). The Martyrdom Index itself can be somewhat unforgiving, though it is generally considered to be accurate. As might be expected the highest MQ is achieved by Jesus, who reaches 26.476. It is impossible, or at least very improbable, to achieve a score much closer to 27 as to do so one would have to die for one's beliefs whilst under the age of eighteen months and yet have had a lasting and emotionally evolutionary impact upon your society. More recently, and in the era of the Artist as spiritual vessel, Christopher Marlowe reaches 18.674, Keats and Shelley both come in at precisely 17.532, with Byron at a staggering 23.689, largely due to his reputation in Greece as a political revolutionary. In the 20th century Elvis Presley scores 17.117, Sid Vicious reaches 22.673, Kurt Cobain makes it to 23.001 and John Lennon surprisingly only achieves

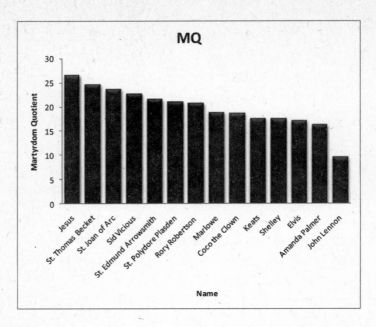

MQ

9.548 as the fact that his death resurrected his career, and not the other way around, is factored into the equation. Amongst the more notable surprises: Coco the Clown (in his most famous incarnation portrayed by Nikolai Poliakov) reaches a most unexpected 18.573, whilst virtually forgotten 1950s children's TV presenter Rory Robertson, who died in an unfortunate incident involving choking and a number of the cuddly toys used in the programme, scores an extraordinary 20.673. This work is generally considered to be the most important foundation text for the student of Doxithanotology.

4. *The Martyrdom Constant*: Le Grenier postulates, in another much remarked-upon work entitled *A Statistical Demonstration of the Matyrdom Constant*, that the total sum of martyrdom quotients in any given society remains constant and is directly proportional to the number of individuals within that society, divided by the number of citizens who live below the Standardised Metric Poverty Line (SMPL). It is worth noting that far from

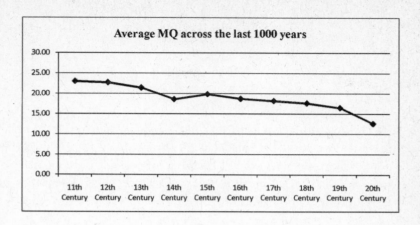

Average MQ across the last 1000 years

being a constant, the *Martyrdom Constant* is in fact a variable. In today's Western civilisation, with an ever-growing population and an unusually high proportion of people living above the SMPL there is a continually increasing social demand for martyrdom, hence the level of attainment required to become an icon, and therefore eligible for the role of martyr, must by necessity fall. This is often cited as an explanation for the obsession with low-brow celebrity culture currently exhibited ad nauseam across both Europe and America. According to the theory this situation is unfortunately self-perpetuating, for as the number of martyrs required by society increases, the easier it must be, by necessity, to attain such a level, thus the average martyrdom quotient falls even lower requiring a greater number of potentials . . . etc., etc. . . . By le Grenier's own admission, the theory ceases to work in any useful way once more than 50% of the given society has become iconic.

Among other of the more interesting volumes to have appeared in recent years there are a number worthy of brief mention here to give a fair impression of the current breadth of the field, and indeed also offered as an general reading list for those interested.

R.S.Kepple's *Contemporary Sin-Eaters* is a serious scholarly study that argues that our consumption of celebrity-death material and willingness to suspend disbelief in the context of celebrity-death scenarios (*Elvis spotted in Bruges* . . . the *Prince Philip-Diana death conspiracy* . . . etc. . . .) is a psychological displacement for the sacrificial instinct, as transposed through the act of communion. In addition it is rich in colourful illustrations and comes with a free CD.

On the more cynical popularist side there is Peter "Soufflé" Merchant's *Cooking with Dead Celebs* which claimed to contain the favourite recipes of many iconically deceased figures. This book makes for a fascinating example of source material. It is basic exploitation literature at its most extreme. After sitting comfortably at no. 2 on the non-fiction bestsellers list for six weeks it was suddenly withdrawn from sale pending litigation by the Estate of Keith Moon over a family recipe for mushroom canapés, quickly followed by a second suit from Hank Marvin arguing that his inclusion in the book was essentially libellous as he was not yet dead. At the time of publication neither case has yet come to court thus no comment can be made here with regard to the outcome.

For further reading the keen student of Doxithanotology should consider Emily Watkinson's *When Death Became Art*, Sir James Melton's *On the Difference Between Death and Art,* and Hilary Jameson-Bowen's epic though inelegantly titled *How, in the Late 20th Century, We Came to Believe that the Destruction of Imagination was the Legitimate Destination of Western Art's Journey from the Renaissance to the Present Day: Discussed.*

There is, in addition, one last and highly controversial theory that, despite considerable reservations amongst the majority of experts in the field, must nonetheless be mentioned in the interest of balance. This is the *Wild Card Proposition*. Originally posited by the once eminent, though now sadly disgraced, German mathematician Leopold Adler, this theory relates to an unexpected idiosyncrasy in the multiple equations used to calculate le Grenier's martyrdom quotient. It had been noticed by many statisticians that where the MQ equals the square-root of a prime number certain subsequent calculations generate confused and inconsistent results. This was initially considered nothing more than a glitch in the system, and was largely irrelevant as in practice an MQ can only be calculated to three decimal places (due to an inevitable lack of pertinent data), thus making the identifying of such cases impossible as most prime number square roots of relevant magnitudes demand at least six decimal places. Adler argued in his paper *Social Manifestations of the Prime-Root MQ* that far from being a glitch, such results indicate a dramatic and unpredictable impact upon society. He cites a number of possible but improvable examples: Jesus comes up with a calculable MQ of 26.476, however, if this could be more accurately calculated we might find the true MQ to be 26.47640459 . . . which is the square root of the prime 701, thus statistically demonstrating a considerable propensity for social impact; likewise, Sir Thomas More comes in at 19.925, which might equate to the square root of 397; Vincent Van Gogh at 16.643 ($\sqrt{277}$?) and Elvis Presley at 17.117 ($\sqrt{293}$?). This argument may seem compelling but it must be borne in mind that he only lists those whom history retrospectively considers arbiters of great social change. By application of the same calculations it could be suggested that Isadora Duncan (a dancer whose trademark scarf became caught in the wheels of a car), or Linda Cleary (a 1940s puppeteer who was accidentally garrotted on stage by one of her puppets during the performance of an adaptation of Lear's *The Quangle Wangle's Hat*) were equally *wild cards*, with all that that implies. In the opinion of the author the *Wild Card Proposition* is nothing more than hopeful speculation on the part of a mathematician desperate to restore his reputation, and should therefore be soundly dismissed as such. However, given the subject of this particular collection of texts it should be noted that Amanda Palmer's MQ has been calculated at 16.217, which may be equal to the square root of prime number 263. Were the *Wild Card Proposition* to be demonstrably true, and were Amanda Palmer's MQ to actually equate with $\sqrt{263}$ we would expect to start seeing the first stirrings of social or artistic change purporting to be in her name or her spirit over the next decade or so. In the past such early stirrings have usually expressed themselves through the growth of cults, new churches and radical artistic movements, however in today's more superficial and materialist culture, and particularly given the current unprecedented speed of global communications, it will be very interesting to see what, if any, form such early expressions take. Indeed it has been suggested by some that the internet-based literary genre of the *palmeresque* is just such an early stirring. Time will tell, however the author of this essay remains sceptical; there should, after all, be no room for "woolly thinking" in the precise science of statistics.

A BRIEF ACCOUNT OF THE DEVELOPMENT
OF THE PALMERESQUE
By Dr. Kyla Dufford

The death of Amanda Palmer on May 13th 2002 passed largely unnoticed by the wider world, initially at least. Certainly there were the usual obituaries in local newspapers, and a few more substantial considerations of her legacy in the international music press, but, given the size and loyalty of her audience, the lack of larger scale media coverage was perhaps a little surprising. This was no doubt due in part to the unfortunate timing: the announcement of her death fell on the same day that a certain female "celebrity" chose to reveal her omission of underwear to photographers whilst exiting a car, thus occupying a great many of the column inches reserved for popular culture commentaries. This lack of press coverage was in addition most likely aggravated by the confusion and uncertainty surrounding the circumstances of her death.

It is known that her body was never found, and the refusal of the police to reveal any further details with regard to the nature of their investigation, combined with the closed inquest, and the coroner's verdict of "unlawful killing" has, over the past few years, inevitably led to all kinds of wild, and in some cases, fantastical speculations. As might be expected under the circumstances, conspiracy theories have abounded. A brief internet search will reveal many blogs and chat-rooms dedicated solely to the discussion of *Who Killed Amanda Palmer?* Most are mundane and involve the US Government attempting to stifle the *Punk-Cabaret* movement due to its dedication to freedom of expression amongst young middle class intellectuals who might otherwise prove useful and productive members of society. However some have proven to be less expected. For example one website (www.wornoutdivas.com) has an extensive blog discussing the proposition that a number of female performers of the previous generation (Madonna, Deborah Harry, Suzi Quatro, Cher, and Linda Ronstadt are all mentioned) may have kidnapped Miss Palmer with the intention of forcibly inducing her to write new "younger" material in an attempt to resurrect their careers.

One of the more interesting conspiracy theories was initially proposed on www.sinnedagainst.tv, and later taken up by many other blogsites. It suggests that Miss Palmer may have been murdered for her ovaries by PAPS (the People's Army Protesting through Song), an organisation dedicated by its own admission to the "creation of a master-race of musicians with the intention of destroying all forms of government and instead uniting the world through the art of song-writing". Deluded as this may sound, it has been alleged that PAPS are responsible for the murders of many female singers around the world, and the subsequent theft of their ovaries, among them the up and coming R&B star LaLa Brown and the Lebanese singer Suzanne Tamim. This rumour gained enough credence for PAPS to release an official statement of denial, although they did admit the illicit aquisition of samples of semen taken from numerous male singer-songwriters through the deceptive misuse of "groupies". In a now notorious 2006 court case brought against them by three un-named male singers PAPS claimed their intention was that of isolating the song-writing gene for future generations. This case was eventually thrown out of court on the grounds that the semen was effectively "given freely in payment for services rendered". None of the girls involved were identified and it is thought that the practice continues. There have of course been, in addition, numerous further theories involving alien abduction, genetic experimentation, time travel, consumption by sasquatch, and others too far-fetched to be worthy of mention.

Given the mysterious circumstances surrounding Miss Palmer's death, it is really neither surprising nor of any great doxithanotological interest that such conspiracy theories have been developed. Indeed, it is only to be expected after the death of a social icon, even when all the details are well known and frankly mundane, and however small their following may be. What has proven to be of much greater interest is the entirely unexpected literary phenomenon that has evolved amongst bloggers following her untimely demise, that being a particular and imaginative form of eulogy that has come to be called the *Palmeresque*. It is not known when this started, nor by whom, as, unfortunately, the web does not leave a paper trail in the conventional sense, thus making the job of the literary historian considerably more difficult. Pages can easily be moved, taken down, copied, and edited, all instantaneously with no accessible way of tracing their history. This does however bring with it certain advantages as once content is put up it frequently finds its way onto innumerable different sites and search engines within days, thus making the sourcing of content itself far easier than was ever the case in the days of pamphlets and newspapers. It is indeed this embracing of the internet, and its influence upon the means and execution of the Palmeresque that sets it apart from other eulogic forms. Whereas today it is common for memorialisations of various types to be expressed through sculpture, the visual arts or music (particularly song), the written memorial has become increasingly rare, and where it does exist it is usually biographical or drunk with praise. The Palmeresque is a different form entirely. Existing exclusively in the unreal and anonymous world of the internet it has embraced this spirit of freedom by casting its sights towards fiction and imagination.

In the last year there have been many interpretations of this effect, both published and unpublished, and much heated debate has been had amongst psychologists, sociologists and literary historians. Conceptual anthropologist Ashley Weldon proposed, in her fascinating paper *The Many-Staged Makings of the Mythological,* that we are seeing in the Palmeresque stage one of an age-old potentially five stage process in which an icon or social figurehead is changed from a human, with all the necessary incumbent weaknesses, to a hero, then a prophet, a messiah and finally in the fifth stage, a god. Of course the last few stages of this process are rarely if ever achieved in the contemporary Western world, (that claim is not made), but the parallel between the Palmeresque and the far-fetched and magical tales that would often spring up after the death of a famous knight or prince in days gone by is indeed worthy of note.

Most pertinent to this publication however is an article by Tabatha Buescher that first appeared in *Sociology Today* and was later developed in the collection *The Socio-Iconic Process: Essays and Introductions* edited by Dr. Cody Ehrman. Buescher turns her analytical eye towards the authors of Palmeresques to consider the motivations that influenced the development of the form:

> . . . To understand why memorialisation takes on any particular form we must first consider not the object, nor the subject, but the needs, requirements and means of those who are effectively the authors of the work. The most common purveyor of memorialisation, that being the State, whose requirement is to demonstrate the perpetual continuity of power and authority, and whose memorials are usually authored by committee, creates bold statements in stone, in the form of statues, buildings and institutions. This is to emphasize permanence, solidity, and a scope greater than that which any individual could muster. The hero may be dead, but their power lives on within the State itself. It is not at all uncommon for such State-financed public memorials to involve the wholesale seizure of iconic figures whose raison d'être was to stand against the very values that they are then used to perpetuate. Probably the most extreme example of this phenomenon in modern times was the ill-considered and short-lived decision to place a statue of John Simon Ritchie (aka Sid Vicious) upon the empty fourth plinth at London's Trafalgar Square. Viewed by many as a cynical attempt by the Mayor of London's office to engage the youth by

honouring its heroes (ironically at least one generation too late), this statue was removed by public demand only three weeks into its intended six month exhibition...

... Among the more interesting non-determined memorial forms to have evolved in recent years are the many writings that began to be distributed over the internet following the death of Amanda Palmer. A popular entertainer of some small note, she had over five years developed an unusually artistic and literate audience due to her flamboyant and somewhat seedy Berlin Cabaret-styled image, and the sophisticated *don't give a damn* attitude expressed through her lyrics. After her premature death, (the mysterious nature of which served only to add considerably to her previously acquired mystique), stories, poems and stream-of-consciousness writings began to appear, first in blogs and chat-rooms, then in other forms of internet-based viral distribution formats such as auto-forwarded emails and Facebook applications etc. . . . These have come to be known as "Palmeresques". Despite covering a wide range of styles and techniques, what all these writings share is a presentation of the continuation of Amanda Palmer: occasionally through her physical survival of Death, but more often through her emotional or spiritual survival, in one form or another. This is in many ways a literal literary representation of the denial of death in what is generally a young and self-consciously artistic demographic, and as such presents many useful insights into the evolving relationship between society, mortality and the Arts . . .

... Let us only hope that the Governor of Massachusetts doesn't bow to current pressure to put up a statue of Palmer outside Boston town hall as has been suggested by certain more cynical members of his legislature...

As stated in the above extract, there are a number of specific qualities that distinguish a Palmeresque from a traditional eulogy. The OED defines a eulogy as "a speech or writing in commendation of the qualities, etc., of a person or thing". The Palmeresque steers clear of praise, focussing instead upon more imaginative responses to Miss Palmer's death. Where a eulogy explicitly looks back over the life of the deceased, the Palmeresque looks forward from the point of death to contemplate either the nature, or further ramifications of her demise. Among the more frequently employed forms are short stories and poems, although letters and stream-of-consciousness explorations are not uncommon. Many seem to be fragmentary, although this could in part be due to the nature of the internet as a medium: any piece of writing of substantial length is inevitably split between online pages and hence when they are copied from one site to another it is not uncommon for parts to go missing, and pages sometimes get deleted leaving only the opening portions available – although in some cases it is impossible to tell whether or not the original may have only been a fragment itself, as is suspected in many examples. One thing that they all share is anonymity. This is particularly interesting as the traditional eulogy, in the popular form of the 17th century, was as much about emphasising a connection between the author and the deceased, thus to bathe in reflected glory, as it was about praise for the dead.

It is this renouncing of authorship that first caught the attention of theoretical psychologist Dr. Stanley Quince whilst conducting a study of motivations towards anonymity, focussing specifically upon the late 20th century. In his colourful 2007 paper *Withdrawings from Authorship – the Internet and the Self* he offers the following paragraph in speculative explanation:

"...The self-named phenomena of the "Palmeresque" clearly demonstrates this tendency towards rebellion through anonymity in the age of the individual, in this case being an artistic expression, more specifically involving the art of *interature*, that brand of literature which has evolved exclusively to service the many unique requirements of the internet. Following the death of Amanda Palmer, a performance artist of moderate success, her uniquely loyal and creative following (a direct result of the unusually theatrical, generous and overall constructive expression of the "don't give a damn" attitude she presented through her music and media profile) intuitively came together at some point to symbiotically evolve a set of rules through which her memory might be celebrated. In this particular context the sense of community might easily have been shattered by any expression of individual ego through claims of authorship, and it is indeed a testament to the general emotional sensitivity of her fans that a consensus of anonymity seems to have been brought about so seamlessly. Finally, by giving a name to their shared aspiration, in this case being the *Palmeresque*, the communal ownership of the medium is asserted and it can be formalised..."

Whatever may be the motivations or inspirations behind the development of the Palmeresque, there is no denying the enthusiasm with which it has been taken up. To date, (September 2008), 6743 distinct and identifiable examples have been catalogued, with a further 1260 being classed as quasi-Palmeresques. By the beginning of 2007 the word itself began to be used outside the context of its original reference to Amanda Palmer. The first known printed use of it in this context comes from a local East London youth film magazine called *Visioning!* In a brief obituary for Ingmar Bergman in their August 2007 edition John Biggs describes the filmmaker (in typically semi-colloquial prose) as "a diamond geezer well worthy of many a Palmeresque". Since then its usage has spread beyond youth culture magazines into the trendier Arts journals, and an entry has now been prepared for the 2010 edition of Butler's Modern English Dictionary, although I and many others would question the accuracy of the proposed definition:

palmeresque [noun]. A piece or fragment of memorial writing, usually fictionalised, which refrains from praise or direct contemplation of the life passed.

ON THE FOUNDING, ASPIRATIONS AND THE FURTHER
INTENTIONS OF THE AMANDA PALMER TRUST (APT)
By Franklin Davey, Executive Chairman of the APT

In September 2006, following the untangling of Miss Palmer's highly complex financial affairs, the Amanda Palmer Trust (APT) was founded with the intention of *working towards the perpetuation and development of the vernacular arts, with specific emphasis upon the weird, freakish and generally other,* as stated in her will. (The actual words in the will were *Fucking Rock Love Art Incarnate* but these were deemed inappropriate for the manifesto of an arts-based charity fund by a vote of 7 to 6 – a decision still considered contentious by some.) To date it has funded, or part-funded, sixteen projects including *Die Hard – An Itch In Time* by *The World's Tiniest Theatre* (a theatrical retelling of the *Die Hard* story portrayed through the medium of the flea circus, unusually in this case using real fleas); *Dead White Music* by record producer Dog-Faced Gimp (a series of recordings from the graves of famous European composers using hydrophones (underwater microphones) pushed six feet into the ground where they lie); and *Suck On This* by Amy Kinsley (explained as a neo-feminist answer to England's Cerne Abbas Giant: this involved the cutting of a 700ft vulva into the chalk downland outside Austin, Texas, with the words *Suck On This* encircling it. The image is only visible from the air, but is directly below one of the busiest flight routes in the US. So far all attempts to remove the image by the Texas authorities have failed. It was supposed to only last one week but is still clearly visible nearly two years on).

Among the first projects taken up by APT was the compiling of a database of *palmeresques*. This task was given initial priority as it was believed that the transitory nature of the internet combined with what at the time was thought to be a short-lived phenomenon implied that they would not be available to catalogue for very long. On both counts this has since proven not to be the case, as neither the viral nature of internet sharing nor the theatrically obsessive nature of Amanda's fans were given great enough credit. Indeed some examples have been found on many thousands of different web pages and it has been estimated that with no further maintenance and given the average natural wastage of web pages and sites it could take 167.34 years for one particularly popular example to no longer be found, although admittedly that figure has been disputed.

In compiling this small and inevitably unrepresentative collection of *palmeresques* many difficult and complex decisions have had to be taken. It was initially agreed that we were not looking for the best examples, if such a quality can even be defined in a web-based viral form, nor the most poignant or sentimental. Along the way various other options were considered: the most varied selection (too many); the most representative (impossible to collate); the most mystifying (this one almost got through); and the most popular (determined by the number of web pages they have been copied to – but this generated too many very similar examples). During the process a considerable amount of debate was expended on what is precisely meant by the term *Fucking Rock Love Art Incarnate*, it was however eventually established that no objective definition could be agreed upon. Finally a consensus of diverse opinions was accepted: each member of the editorial committee would choose their own example, and write a single page introduction explaining the reasons behind this choice (So as not to effectively provide spoilers these introductions will be placed at the end of each story, and will thus be entitled "extroductions".) Given the large number of texts requiring due consideration, a problem further compounded by the fact that many of them share very similar titles, it was decided that the catalogue would be randomly divided into ten groups which would then, again randomly, be divided amongst the ten editors. Additionally, and in sympathy with the spirit of the *palmeresque*, these editors, and their extroductions, agreed to remain anonymous.

Regardless of literary merit, and this may indeed be found wanting in some if not many cases, it is important to consider whilst reading the following texts the nature of what is actually being read. These stories, poems and fragments were never intended for physical publication, but were written out of a need for catharsis, an expression of grief, and most of all, to honour a soul that is sorely missed. What makes them interesting, and worthy of presentation to a wider public is the phenomenon, and indeed the very existence, of the *palmeresque* itself.

Franklin Davey.

A BRIEF NOTE ON THE CHOICE OF ILLUSTRATIONS

Given the aural and visual nature of Miss Palmer's work, and indeed the much demonstrated audio-visual creativity of her fanbase, it might be expected that the virtual space inhabited by the *palmeresque* would abound with songs, music and pictures, however, it is interesting to note, and much commented upon, that the phenomenon of the *palmeresque* appears only in the form of the written word. Many theories have been put forward to explain this unexpected literary bias, and, if interested, a useful summary can be found in Dr. Francesca Morrison's 2007 paper "Grief, Hysteria and Creative Ambiguity". In essence she concludes that:

> . . . *where music and the visual arts both demand a direct and immediate emotional response, words are by their very nature kept at a distance and must be considered, understood and interpreted by the conscious mind, allowing for the expression of more complex emotional issues such as those inspired by grief for a symbol which, in essence, represents an aspect of the self.*

Whatever the explanation our original intention of illustrating this book with appropriate *palmeresque* images, anonymously posted online by fans, was not to be, as none could be found, despite the wealth of fan-art posted online during Miss Palmer's lifetime. However it was agreed that the book should definitely be illustrated, if only to entice the more easily daunted reader. Thus, after much discussion, it was decided to open the commission for illustrations to tender, more specifically to ten up-and-coming young artists, each of whom could claim some personal, aesthetic or emotional link to Miss Palmer herself, and/or her works.

After a month or so we had ten submissions from ten artists and were left with the difficult process of deciding how we might make the final choice. Initially it was proposed that we should let the fans make the decision, although this proved to be impractical. We did however agree that it should be some symbolic representation of Miss Palmer's fan-base that made the choice, and so, by way of compromise, settled upon asking the teenage and pre-teen daughters of members of the Executive Committee. However, there was some concern that, by the age of thirteen, such girls may have acquired their own entirely separate agenda, as is all too often the case, and so, finally, we agreed to leave the choice in the hands of daughters of the Executive Committee aged eight to twelve. Thus the decision ultimately fell to ███████████, aged nine, daughter of our Chief Catering Manager, who has asked to be identified as the Picture Editor.

We at the APT are particularly happy with the final choice of celebrated up-and-coming West Coast artist Karli Young, whose work was chosen, in ██████████'s own words, because "it's cute, and a little bit scary" – both qualities we feel could have been equally applied to Miss Palmer herself.

FRANKLIN DAVEY

TEXT NUMBER ONE

On the Dancing Death of Amanda Palmer

When Amanda Palmer ran away from the circus she knew that that would not be the end of it. Indeed it was the wrong circus to run away from. But then again, it was the wrong circus to be brought up by, though that hadn't really been her choice. She had been stolen from her family when she was only four, and could remember nothing of her previous life except her name. Nor would they tell her anything, not even which town she had been taken from. What she didn't know was that she had been the youngest of twelve children, to a very poor family, and when her parents had eventually noticed she was missing they saw it as something of a relief. No, she was a circus girl, and that was the end of it. And so it might have been had she not grown up. For though they had bullied and beaten her almost every day of her life, she had become used to that, even found it oddly comforting. It wasn't until her budding womanhood began to show through her shirt that the real problems began.

Silas Monger's Travelling Circus was a family troupe that had toured the northern states for seven generations. Indeed they had utilised the careful management of "in-breeding" very much to their advantage over the centuries. Not that they were freaks, well, not really. But they were the weirdest looking circus you were ever likely to come across. The clowns, who were all dwarfs, and cousins come to that, were of generally normal proportions for such diminutive folk, but had the most enormous ears and noses, giving them something of the look of baby elephants, particularly when crawling on all fours; the strong man, who was, as might be imagined, immensely strong, had such elongated arms that he could almost pick up his weights without bending; and the stilt-walkers were exceptionally tall, a good foot taller than any among the crowds even without their stilts. But despite this dedication towards the blood purity of the circus line, as they called it, the past two generations had seen a steady decline in their prosperity, and for the last twenty years they had been reduced to playing highway services and the occasional small town.

It was for this reason that Silas Monger VIII had declared that they must break with tradition and bring in some new blood, and hence they had stolen Amanda. However, little thought had been given, or at least little discussion been had, as to who else's blood might be going into the mix. Silas assumed that it would be his, but many among the troupe had other ideas, all of them male, fertile, without wives, and, truth to be told, in most cases diseased as a result of various sordid liaisons with the less salubrious professionals that shared the same passing trade. Naturally Amanda was oblivious to all this for many years. She was more concerned with keeping her head down and ensuring her chores were done to avoid a thorough beating. But then, as she approached her thirteenth year, the rising self-consciousness of impending adulthood began to turn her thoughts, and almost overnight she started noticing the way that they looked at her. Though she didn't understand quite why, it made her flesh creep, of that much she was sure. And then there were the cold and savage glances sent her way by the women of the troupe, particularly Evelyn and Evelyn, the singing conjoined twins (their father had given them the same name so as to avoid confusion) and so she kept her head down, and did her chores with even greater vigour so as not to provide the opportunity for any unwanted attentions.

The only comfort and companionship she ever experienced

was in her relationship with the animals. These were two donkeys, and an old panther, whose teeth were falling out. When she was first taken she had been made to sleep in the animal tent, which was little more than a makeshift tarpaulin awning on the side of the donkey trailer to cover the panther's rusting cage. Not having seen a panther before she assumed it was just a big pussycat and before long she was sleeping in his cage, cuddling up to him for warmth. She named him Fluffy, after all she was only four. It always caused her great inward amusement to see how Fluffy would spit and hiss at the rest of the troupe, and how scared they were of him, though she never let them see it, for that would just have led to another beating. But to her he was quite literally a pussycat.

In the months running up to her fifteenth birthday she could tell something was brewing, something that wasn't good. Her nights were increasingly disturbed by shouts, arguments, and even fistfights amongst the troupe, and the looks she was getting had become ever more accusatory. Then, two nights before her birthday she was rudely awoken from a particularly pleasant dream involving a large pink feathered hat, by an argument heading her way. She was too groggy to understand what was being shouted, but it seemed to quickly turn into a fight, and then silence. Suddenly the door to Fluffy's cage was flung open and a hand grabbed her ankle and was dragging her out. It was Hector, the strong man. She tried to kick and scream with all her might, but to no avail. His hands were just too big and too strong. Before she knew it she was over his shoulder, being carried off. But Hector had forgotten to close Fluffy's cage. There was an almighty hissing screaming sound as Fluffy leapt up at Hector's face, clamping his toothless jaws around the unsuspecting man's nose. In no time Hector was on the ground, wrestling the fearsome beast that Fluffy seemed to have become, and Amanda saw her chance. She ran, just ran and ran straight across the fields into the darkness, and kept on running until her lungs ached and her heart seemed to be bursting forth from her chest. Finally she felt safe enough to stop, and simply lay on the ground among the corn stems, waiting for daylight, wondering what she should do now.

****

With Amanda gone Monger's circus rapidly went from bad to worse. They hadn't realised it at the time, but it was her who had held the ragged troupe together. With her arrival she had brought to their claustrophobic inward looking world a sticky spider's web of hope, lust and jealously that had managed to distract them from the evident final decline of their profession, binding them together with a promise of better times to come. The women had stopped bitching amongst each other to share a mistrust and jealousy of the new girl. The men had all secretly prized the fantasy of taking her as their wife. In short, they had needed her and indeed Silas Monger VIII had suspected this all along. Now she was gone the in-fighting began again with renewed vigour. Silas had lost his authority, and with it his circus had lost its consensus. They hadn't moved on since that fateful night, and within weeks their little community was falling apart.

One night, Hector, who had not forgotten his humiliation at the claws of the toothless Fluffy, resolved to kill the beast, but being somewhat the worse for drink had only managed to open the cage door when he was once again knocked to the ground, this time breaking his wrist. Fluffy disappeared into the surrounding darkness never to be seen again. Shortly after this the fights started. At first these were isolated events between individuals, but before long the situation had escalated out of hand into what can only be described as all out war between the various acts. Had an unsuspecting traveller stumbled upon the troupe during that final fight, they would have thought themselves dreaming, or on drugs. Indeed the mêlée was more than a little surreal. The four dwarf clowns, two of them mounted upon scrawny donkeys, ambushed the stilt-walkers and the two Evelyns as they sat plotting their takeover, bringing down the tent upon their heads, then circling it with ropes in an attempt to bag them and drag them into the surrounding ditch. However this plan was not well judged, and one of the immensely tall stilt-walkers managed to wriggle his way free, grabbed the two pedestrian dwarfs by the legs and swung them around his head before sending them flying through the air into the surrounding fields. Meanwhile the collapsed tent had caught fire, and by the time the Evelyns had escaped its entanglement their hair and clothes were all dreadfully singed and they ran screaming around the encampment for water. Hector, who had broken his ankle in a previous drunken brawl in addition to his wrist, came hobbling out of his tent to see what was going on, only to be run down by the dwarf-laden donkeys. Silas himself, however, had taken a number of sleeping pills and remained completely unaware of the ensuing chaos that surrounded the caravan he shared with his mother, Lavenia, the circus fortune teller. Lavenia was stone deaf and never had any trouble sleeping.

As Silas emerged from his caravan shortly after sunrise the following morning his heart broke to see the wreckage of all that his family had worked towards for so many years. The camp had been destroyed, the animals gone, and the troupe itself was battered and bewildered. They sat, in diverse little groups around the camp, bandaged and scarred, united only in the look of despair and bitterness upon their faces.

Silas did all he could in a vain attempt to unite them once again. He gave the best speech of his life, filled with promises no one could possibly keep, and many brilliant comic asides, but all to no avail. Before the sun was fully overhead the troupe had packed up the wreckage of seven generations and dispersed. Silas and his mother were all that remained of Monger's Circus.

As they sat on the porch of their caravan, looking out across the remnants of the previous night's carnage, and drinking coffee out of charred tin cans, Lavenia lectured Silas on all he had done wrong, in her view, as she did most mornings. And, as he did most mornings, Silas sat there, faking a kindly smile whilst calling her all manner of names, many of which a son should never call a mother, in the full knowledge that she was deaf as a doorpost, and had never learnt to read lips. But underneath this touching scene, darker thoughts were simmering. They both knew who was really to blame, who was really responsible for the destruction of all that their family had worked towards over so many generations: Amanda. It was all down to Amanda. And that is when it happened. That is when the curse was invoked, for the Mongers were a gypsy family, well-versed in the execution of a wide range of curses. But that curse, the dancing curse, that was something special, reserved only for the most deserving of perpetrators, and hadn't been cast since the days of Silas' grandmother.

* * * *

Without wishing to give away the means and execution of such a powerful invocation, for that would indeed be most irresponsible and may well lay me open to the wrath of many a gypsy family who have kept this secret safe, I will summarise its content and effect: in simple terms, if Amanda were to ever experience a single moment of true happiness she would be seized by the overwhelming urge, nay need, to dance, and to never stop dancing. She would dance in every conscious waking moment for the rest of her life, until her body lay broken by exhaustion, and her mind was destroyed by the fitful fever of the dancing madness. A cruel and evil curse indeed, though for now there was no danger of it taking effect. Amanda was lost, confused and had no idea how the outside world worked. A more scared and pitiable figure would be hard to find.

* * * *

It was a long journey from the barren wastes of the Midwest to Boston, and seemed that at every stage Amanda was accompanied by the most extraordinary luck, as if all the good fortune that had evaded her so far in life had finally caught up with its intended recipient and fell upon her in one moment. As everyone who lives in the real world would know, a fifteen year old girl dressed only in a night-shirt, wandering alone along isolated desert roads might well find herself in all kinds of trouble, but Amanda seemed blessed. At every encounter, every pickup that passed, every small town along the way she seemed to inspire nothing but the kindness of strangers. By the time she arrived in Boston two weeks later she had acquired a full set of warm clothes and enough money to keep her body and soul in healthy union for quite some time. Why had she headed to Boston? She wasn't really sure, but she had heard it was a beautiful town, and a good long way from the touring routes followed by the Mongers, and that was all she needed.

Her luck seemed to stay with her. A few days after her arrival she had been befriended by the ragtag community of street performers who arrived each morning around Faneuil Hall Marketplace, and set about making herself useful with her many skills for the maintenance and repair of their circus apparel and equipment. Her flair for designing the fantastical did not go unappreciated and before long she had her own pitch, and was making good money as a living statue, dressed in an ever more spectacular array of bizarre and exotic costumes.

* * * *

Her steady rise from living statue to international singing superstar has been well documented in many places. A cursory search of the internet will reveal the path this journey took in far more detail than can possibly be included here, so in the interest of brevity, and short attention spans, my own included, let us jump to that fateful evening in February 2006 when it seemed she had achieved the impossible, and alas, her happiness was, for the first time in her life, entirely uncontained.

* * * *

There she was, standing on the stage of Carnegie Hall, taking in the applause like a drug. She had made it, all the way, to the very top. Was it possible that the frail little circus girl of old was actually here? As she bathed in the glory and adoration of 3000 hysterical fans the great weight of insecurity she had carried with her since childhood finally fell away and she could feel the joy of it all pooling in her belly. She was entirely overwhelmed and could no longer contain herself.

It started with her toes, gently tapping within her shoes. Then her feet began to move, only small gestures at first, barely visible across the vast expanse of the hall, but before long she was leaping and twirling in a manner not quite befitting the situation. After some minutes the applause began to dissipate, to be replaced by an air of puzzlement and confusion. The situation was momentarily rescued by the quick thinking of the drummer who came forward, took a second bow himself engendering a resurgence of applause, and then gently led the frantically dancing Amanda off the stage. As the audience slowly dissipated this peculiar conclusion to the show was soon forgotten amidst the exited babble of high spirits after a most enthralling evening's entertainment. But for Amanda, poor Amanda, the compulsion to dance seemed unstoppable. She was completely unable to change out of her stage clothes or even remove the thick white makeup that had become her trademark. All she could do was dance, dance and dance again.

The hours passed as her roadies packed up the sets and in-struments, but still Amanda danced, a look of fear and fatigue steadily growing upon her face. Once everything was stowed in its proper place it was decided that they should carry her to the tour-coach and deliver her to her hotel room. By then it was clear that exhaustion was taking hold, and her movements had become increasingly violent and erratic. A doctor was called, sedatives were administered, but still Amanda danced on. It wasn't until early evening the following day that her movements finally calmed as at last she sank into a deep restorative sleep.

She must have slept for a good 16 hours but then as she woke the next morning, before she even had a chance to consider what might have happened, her toes began to tingle, then twitch, and the whole process began again. And so it continued, day after day, occasionally punctuated by long periods of sleep that served only to recharge her body for the next onslaught on dancing. She was taken to her home, a large house and garden in Brookline, and a nurse was employed to feed her by drip and bandage her swollen, bruised and bloodied feet as she slept, but still the dancing continued. Doctors were called, specialists brought in, even a retired anthropologist who had spent years studying the dancing pygmies of Namibia, but all to no avail.

Of course all of this cost money, and lots of it, and despite her blossoming stardom her income was considerably depleted along the way by the many demands made upon it by record labels, agents, managers, producers, co-writers, ghost-writers, and all the other numerous hangers-on who had slowly inveigled their way into her inner circle, or at least into access to her bank balance. Without the ability to earn, for it was naturally impossible to sing, to perform, record, to give interviews or even run a business whilst being compelled to ceaselessly dance, it was not long before her funds began to shrink, and with them went much of her staff and, sadly, a fair number of her friends. As further months passed even the more loyal amongst her friends became tired of the continual concern and visits became infrequent. Finally the money ran dry, her house was listed for foreclosure, the nurse discharged herself of her duties, and it seemed as if Amanda might be left to slowly die of exhaustion and malnutrition, for she had no family to fall back upon, nobody to care for her, she was entirely alone.

Or so she thought.

* * * *

Lavenia had died a week after the dancing started, but she had sensed that it had begun, and left Silas detailed instructions on how to proceed. Thus on the six month anniversary of his mother's death Silas Monger VIII made his way to Mill Dam Road just in time to see Amanda cast from her house, and stand in the street dancing both aimlessly and with considerable vigour, tears rolling down her thinly drawn cheeks as the last of her furniture was repossessed. Once again she had nowhere to go, no one to turn to, but this time her luck seemed to have deserted her.

She had no idea what to do. In her current state she couldn't even approach a stranger or official for help. A doctor or policeman would take one look at her and have her put away for good in the loony bin. She wouldn't be able to explain who she was or what had happened. She couldn't even talk as she was constantly out of breath with the effort, let alone write. She was utterly and entirely lost and helpless.

"Amanda? . . ." She recognised the voice and spun around in a clumsy and clearly unmotivated pirouette. Yes, it was Silas. She tried to speak but instead found herself waltzing around him in erratic circles.

"Come with me Amanda, we can sort this out . . ." It was the best offer she had, indeed it was the only offer, and strangely, she found his presence almost reassuring, even comforting, in this most exceptional and difficult of circumstances. And so she went with him, for better and for worse, little aware of the tragic consequences that were shortly to unfold. Had she not, there is no doubt that her fate would have been equally dreadful, for she had become the very definition of being trapped between a rock and a hard place, and she was falling.

* * * *

Silas Monger VIII soon discovered he had a flair for publicity. Why this had never come forth before he didn't know. Maybe it was his mother's watchful eye that had curtailed him, for it is undeniable that strange things can happen to folk when their parents die. All manner of hidden talents and abilities hitherto undreamt of may reveal themselves at last without the fear of condemnation. And in Silas' case, this was a gift for playing the media; afterall he had a commodity on his hands, a saleable one at that. He announced in all the newspapers that international singing star Amanda Palmer was *Dancing for Peace,* and that she wouldn't cease her dance until every nation worldwide had laid down its arms in conciliation. This seemed a safe bet, as he knew she wouldn't stop dancing, and equally, the world was unlikely to stop fighting, yet who could deny the worthiness of such a gesture. And indeed he was right. The story caught the imagination of every news network in America and many across Europe and Asia. TV appearances abounded, although naturally Silas did all the interviews: Amanda was merely wheeled on (often literally) to dance in the background as he spoke eloquently on the subject of international diplomatic relations. He arranged dance-a-thons in all the major cities across the States, and thousands turned up to *Dance for Peace* with Amanda. He produced t-shirts, music boxes, little plastic nodding Amandas, and all manner of kitsch and tat with Amanda's image and the *Dancing for Peace* logo printed upon it, which were sold at vastly inflated prices to an eager market. And even her records began to sell again. Naturally Silas, as her adoptive father and business manager had full control of the money, and spent it with considerable enthusiasm, for he had never been rich before. He developed an excessive and largely uninformed taste for the finer things in life, though he did at least invest some money in more practical acquisitions, such as a compound in Malibu with three outbuildings, and a fleet of trucks and busses for touring the *Amanda Palmer Dance-a-thon,* which had by then become a show in its own right. Amanda herself was well catered for, under the circumstances. She had her own trailer, of not inconsiderable size, and a full team of nurses and makeup artists on hand to ensure she looked and felt at least relatively healthy. More than that she would have no use for in her current state. And given that she would be dancing on regardless, dancing for Peace didn't seem such a bad thing to be doing.

The real hubbub lasted about six months with a seemingly endless stream of requests for TV and radio appearances, and she even made it onto page three of *Time* magazine. Then the media coverage began to wane, but Silas seized the moment to announce the *Dancing for Peace* world tour, and there was a second flurry of publicity. But he knew it couldn't last, for Madame Fame is an impatient, flippant and cruel mistress; that knowledge was in his blood. And sure enough within 18 months the crowds were thinning out, the merchandise piling up, and it became financially unviable to keep the show on the road. The sets were put into storage and Amanda's trailer was parked up in the Malibu compound.

There was still a small audience keen to see her dance, and not being a man to kick a gift-horse in the behind, Silas set about milking what little he could from it. He had a small stage erected in the compound and road signs put up across Southern California declaring *Amanda Is Still Dancing* plus an arrow to direct passing trade their way. Whenever a car pulled up Amanda would be placed on the stage to dance for them, for the meagre fee of $50. Silas had explained that if he was keep employing the two remaining nurses that kept her fed and cared for her by now painfully disfigured feet, she had to keep earning whenever the opportunity arose. Meanwhile Silas turned his attention to his next main attraction: a parrot called General George that could recite the entire Bill of Rights. He planned to market it as the reincarnation of George Washington.

A year passed and the visitors became ever more infrequent. Amanda took to spending much of her time dancing in the fields around the compound. One day she came upon Fluffy's old cage, buried under a pile of crates and tarpaulins in a ditch, and had it moved next to her trailer, and an awning put up over it. There she would sleep between the dancing frenzies, and dream of her childhood. But by now her body was worn and her feet were barely functional. Over the past year she had received too many fractures and her spine had slowly become crooked from exertion. She knew she couldn't keep this up for much longer, and perhaps that would really be a blessing.

Then one morning, shortly after the dancing began she felt an immense pain shoot up her right leg as her achilles tendon snapped. She fell to the ground but continued flailing for the compulsion to dance was still burning within despite her body's inability. Silas found her rolling in the courtyard and had her carried back to the cage. The nurses gathered to see what could be done, but it was agreed in whispered tones that the cost of all the necessary surgeries to her feet, legs and spine would be prohibitive. Within a week Silas decided to let the nurses go. A few days later a car pulled up and paid the requisite $50. Silas had the cage moved onto the stage for their entertainment but the spectacle of Amanda writhing and jerking upon her back disturbed more than it amused and so he had a blanket put over it and ordered the road signs taken down.

By now General George was becoming a star and had been offered a part in the latest *National Treasure* movie. Naturally Silas's entire entourage went along to enjoy the Hollywood glamour, and thus Amanda was forgotten. No one knew when she died, but upon their return she was found to be still, her twisted broken body contorted beyond recognition, and yet there was the smallest shadow of a smile stretched across her drawn and emaciated face, perhaps a look of relief, or even revelation.

Her death was widely reported, and Silas sold the film rights to her life story for a record figure. Many newspapers described her as a martyr to the cause of world peace, and a motion for a day of international pan-global ceasefire was even proposed at the UN in honour of her efforts, although it had no chance of actually being ratified.

She was cremated at the Jonah Crematorium, Malibu, on Friday May 13th, 2002, and Silas had the larger bone fragments mounted as relics in Perspex blocks, on the off-chance that she might be canonised at some point in the future. The smaller ashes he had baked into cookies and sold on Ebay to her remaining fans, with one reaching over $500. No stone was ever placed to her memory. Today all that remains of Amanda Palmer is her recordings, which can still occasionally be heard on light music radio stations around the world, and, from time to time, might even inspire someone to get up and dance, confident in the knowledge that they can stop whenever they wish.

A Personal Extroduction from Text Number One

By ███████████

Having read through nearly eight hundred texts it is clear to me that the phenomenon of the *palmeresque* is more interesting than the many individual writings themselves, for most, at least amongst the selection I was given, seem to be very similar and seep that brand of two-dimensional fan adoration that has always made me feel a little queasy. That said, there were a number of texts that stood out for various reasons, and in this case it was both the quality of the writing and the parabolic (in both senses of the word) nature of the storyline.

Strictly speaking this text is more a quasi-*palmeresque*, as it breaks a number of the notional rules, most obviously in its presentation of the means of Amanda's death, however, since all the biographical content is imagined, and her death is portrayed as a poetical conclusion to the storyline, I was able to convince others amongst the editorial committee that it should be included. In addition, it is one of the few texts that I read to which there is an underlying and meaningful theme.

To my mind this tale is clearly a parable of media celebrity and PR in which Amanda becomes the helpless victim of a savage and brutal machine. In reality this was far from the case: she was well-versed in playing the media, and only on a handful of occasions did the machine get the better of her, but again, it is this reinvention of Amanda as a symbol of powerlessness fallen into the hands of an evil Svengali figure that gives the story a freshness, at least when compared to the other more adoring texts.

Structurally it forms an elegant arc, remarkably akin in many details to the sonata form in classical music. It is effectively built of three acts, beginning and ending in much the same place, with a fairytale rise and decline in between. This concern with formal devices is further emphasized by the placement of its centre: that being the first piece of spoken quoted text, when Silas meets Amanda for the second time, which falls precisely at the golden section, (A+B is to A as A is to B), a structural device often used by classical composers such as Haydn or Mozart. This cannot be mere coincidence and I therefore would suggest that the author was something of a scholar in the formal study of Classical music.

I recognise many references to popular culture TV shows, whether conscious or unconscious on the part of the author. Most striking is the curse itself which is clearly inspired by a gypsy curse from the show *Buffy the Vampire Slayer* and the opening scenes are distinctly reminiscent of *Carnivale*. Finally, as the tale draws to a close I cannot help but be reminded of Kafka's *The Hunger Artist*. Yet all the pieces are neatly sewn together and the story, to my mind, comes across effectively as a whole.

Certainly it is flawed, and there are some passages that read somewhat clumsily, but overall it was the best of a moderate and at times disappointing bunch. Indeed, if it had only been written with a more insightful eye and greater mastery of language it might have been a short story worthy of some note in its own right.

TEXT NUMBER TWO

On the Strange Case of the Death of Amanda Palmer

Amanda Palmer, a singer of some renown, and composer of numerous charming ditties, was midway through her 32nd year when she reluctantly accepted the post of Musician in Residence at St. Mary's School for Girls, near Warrensburg, on the edge of Adirondack Park Preserve. She had, of course, held more prestigious posts in her time, indeed once she had been the very toast of the boards, but, alas, her many benign eccentricities had somewhat gathered momentum over the past few years, and, truth to be told, her reputation was not what it had been. For, Amanda Palmer had a number of unfortunate habits, not least of which was her insistence upon seeing things that weren't quite there, or rather, as she liked to put it, things that other people chose not to see. "The mind reigns over the eyes in all matters of interpretation," she would often declare when challenged, though this somewhat cryptic explanation only served to add to her reputation as a mild-mannered madwoman, although admittedly not without some talent. When pressed further, which was truly a rare occurrence, she would often quote Swedenborg or William Blake, but by that time no one was ever paying her any serious attention, and she often felt that her most enlightening remarks fell upon deaf ears. As with her music.

Certainly she was an averagely adequate singer and pianist, very capable of stringing together a charming, if at times derivative, melody, but her career had never gone quite as she had imagined it should. And after that unfortunate incident at her last major show, which is best left unmentioned here, she had found herself to have run out of options. It was as a personal favour to her father (a rather unpleasant and ill-tempered man who despised his daughter and was more concerned with his own reputation) that her Aunt Elizabeth, head mistress of St. Mary's had offered her a post; Elizabeth's reluctance having been overcome by the generous donation offered to the school in return. However, she was certainly not going to give her any opportunity for direct contact with her girls, and so her new post required only that she performed a concert, once a month, to include some original material, in the Chapel, thus leaving her ample time for contemplation, meditation, confabulation and other appropriate pursuits for a lady. And so it was that she took to strolling across the hills of an afternoon, somewhat against the advice of the locals, for she had never much cared for advice, and still less for locals come to that, and the hills seemed to her to be the perfect place for gathering oneself, for they were free from unmannerly distractions, and the many tedious interruptions she had so often been faced with when living closer to alleged civilisation. There she was able to open her mind to the gentle rhythm of her strolling feet and wander freely, both within and without, unravelling endless melodies in her mind from which she would cherry-pick for her next month's concert. And so it was that she found herself once again out upon the hills one Friday afternoon, three days after her 33rd birthday.

Having taken a slightly different choice of paths than usual, and not having paid any particular heed to her course, as she felt she knew her way quite well enough, she was surprised to find herself entering a narrow wooded valley that she had never come upon before. Admittedly a little excited by this delightful and private discovery, and never having been one to leave an interesting stone unturned, or so she liked to think, she immediately headed down the valley and in among the trees. And what extraordinary trees they were! Though obviously ancient, and being made up mainly of oak, they were all fantastically knurled and twisted, and not one of them stood much more than three times her height. Every branch was peeling with long ribbons of lichen reaching down in some cases all the way to the boulder strewn ground, from which sprang a veritable jungle of pink and purple foxgloves and giant ferns, making her passage more than a little difficult at times. Finally, having clambered a good fifty yards, aided considerably by the affectation of her walking cane, she came upon a tidy little path gently sloping down the hill. Most extraordinary of all, along the sides of the path every twenty yards or so were what could only be gravestones, roughly hewn from that same granite as the boulders further up the hill. "This is all most perplexing," she thought as she followed the path downwards, "for why would people go to the trouble of burying their dead all the way out here?" There were no obvious signs of habitation, and the graves, though old, were not ancient. Indeed a number of them seemed to be almost recent, judging by the lack of mossy growth upon their faces.

She approached one such stone, set back from the path by about six feet, and nearly fell as her cane became wedged between two rocks. Having regained both her balance and her dignity she swished away at the somewhat overlarge ferns surrounding it with the tip of her cane, until enough was cleared for her to peer forward and inspect it properly. Yes, it did indeed seem to be fairly recent, as the tool marks were still clearly visible and un-eroded, and there were only the occasional spots of lichen, no bigger than a single cent. There were no dates, just a name, which at first she could not make out as her own shadow was blocking the thin residual sunlight that managed its way through the trees. But as she moved to the side she could just about read the words: "Toby Jameson."

"I know that name," she thought. "Now who was it?" and she made her way back to the path. "Yes that's right", she mumbled to herself. "Toby Jameson!" She remembered a boy, no more than twelve, with long blonde locks and a tight purple velvet jacket. Toby had been two years her senior at St. Peters, her old school. He had been a fine pianist, by children's standards anyway, and it was his example that had ultimately inspired Amanda to take up music professionally all those years ago. She recalled that he had managed to grow an unusually confident moustache for a twelve year old. "Still," she thought, "it's not at all an uncommon name. Must be someone else," and she continued her musing as she proceeded on with her stroll. But curiosity soon got the better of her, and before she knew it she was once again struggling over boulders to inspect another gravestone.

Now this one was definitely a little older, being altogether smoother, considerably more worn, and largely covered with a thick coat of moss, which she poked and scratched at with her cane until the face was more or less visible. Again, just a name with no date. She cleared the remaining mossy growth with her fingers and leant in close. What she read sent a distinct and some-what unpleasant thrill along her spine: "Sxip Shirey." Now that had been the name of her Professor at the Academy, whom she knew to be dead and buried in New York's Greenvale Cemetery, as she had personally attended the funeral a few years past. But what a truly extraordinary coincidence. It sent her heart racing, just a little.

By now curiosity had certainly got the better of her and she hurried from stone to stone, paying scant attention to anything bar the names: Evelyn Evelyn, Benjamin Folds, Baby Dee St. Vin-cent: and with each name she read she became a little less curious and a little more afeared, for each and every stone bore the name someone she had known, someone who had, in one way or an-other cast their influence over her life. Certainly she had seen many strange things in her time, and believed in them all, some-times against her better judgement, but none had been so sinister and truly bizarre as this. Further and further down the path she raced, slashing her cane before her at the ferns on either side, in a manner that can only be described as somewhat frenzied. Her mind was whirring. This was impossible! It simply could not be!

She knew it not to be. And yet it was. Here in front of her. Solid as the very stones on which the names were carved. And then, suddenly, something caught her ear, something beautiful, yet strangely unreal, coming from further down the valley. She stopped and listened intently. Yes, it was a voice, an extraordinary voice whose tone surpassed all depth and sweetness of any she had heard. Her mind was in such confusion, and her heart pounding away so fiercely that sheer instinct for safety and survival made her stop in her tracks, and her thoughts retreated into the wondrous sound allowing her frantic body a brief moment of respite.

"What a beautiful song," she thought, and yet she could not place it. It was somehow at once both intimately familiar and enchantingly exotic – perhaps something that she had not heard since her childhood. Yet, it sounded modern, even new, and had a freshness about it that seemed entirely relevant to her at that moment, like freshly picked flowers.

She knew by then that it was inevitable that she should follow the sound, and all conscious and sensible thought left her, for were she to think about what was happening, even for a moment, she would surely become completely mad. And so she followed the path, at a regular and even pace, as if this were the most ordinary of afternoons, as if it were mere idle curiosity that drew her onwards towards the source of the music.

Further and further down the valley she went, and with each step the light seemed to fade just a little, and the strange music seemed to grow ever louder. Finally, after what felt to her like an age (and yet how could she tell, as her mind was entirely confused by now) she approached a small clearing at the very centre of the wood, which she instinctively knew to be the end of the path. And there, stood before another large gravestone, this one freshly carved and slightly glinting in the remnants of the light, was a figure, perhaps a girl, singing to herself, with a voice more magical than could possibly be dreamt of. Amanda stopped. Yes, it was a girl, that much was clear now, slender and petite, though something was unaccountably strange and unreal about her. It was hard to tell anything more, as the evening shadows were creeping in ever closer now, and she appeared only in silhouette. As Amanda listened, entirely enraptured, she suddenly realised, with a momentary gasp, that this phantom, for phantom it surely was, this phantom was staring directly at her as she sang. And yet, though still very much afraid, the music was so sublime, so entirely right in every way, that all Amanda could do was to stand and listen with her mouth hanging slightly open somewhat in the manner of a fool.

How long she stood there is impossible to know, as time no longer existed for her; the world no longer existed; all there was the song; and what a song! It was not a song to be found in this world, but a song as she had dreamed a song could be, a song that had touched the very soul of God and now drifted down to earth as a mirror of His divine intentions.

It seemed that day turned to night and night turned to day and still the phantom girl sang on; and still Amanda listened as the notes unravelled in endless strings of jewels, each one shaped and polished to perfection. Until finally, finally the phrases leant towards an end, the pulse was slowed, the effort subdued, and the wondrous other-worldly music reached its right conclusion.

In the silence that followed Amanda slowly awakened from her reverie, no longer afraid, but burning with awe and admiration. Phantom or no, there was so much she wanted to ask this girl, so much that she wanted to say herself, for surely anyone, anything, that could sing like that was a true Artist and companion soul.

She took a step towards the beshadowed figure and was about to speak when the phantom herself broke the silence.

"So you have come at last", she said. "I have been waiting." It was the strangest voice she had ever heard, almost as if it were not sounded at all, but cast directly into her mind. She was not sure how to respond and stammered without due thought:

"Who are you? . . . What was that song? . . . It was Divine! . . . I myself am a singer you know."

She still could not see the figure clearly as the shadows seemed to follow and emulate her every gesture. Again the phantom spoke:

"It was the song of your life; the music you have been seeking; the music you yourself might have written had your heart and ears remained open!"

Not having fully digested this last statement, Amanda continued:

"Is it written down? . . . Can I get a copy? . . . I would so love to sing it at my next concert."

"That music was for you only, and no one else. Now you have found it your journey has come to an end. It is time to take your place." And with that the phantom stepped from in front of the gravestone, indicating with her hand that the inscription should be read. It was freshly carved with sharp edges catching the light, and the engraved letters, which had been painted in gold, were clearly visible even from the small distance at which Amanda stood. What she read filled her head with horror and her heart with resignation. Inscribed in Gothic lettering were the two words: "Amanda Palmer." As she looked back at the phantom the shadows seemed to clear and all of a sudden she could see the face clearly. It was her own face, her own eyes looking directly back at her, and at last she understood.

More than that I cannot say, for I am only at liberty to report her journey in this world. Her body was never found. And it was supposed by some that she had inadvertently strayed and sunk into a bog.

She was missed by few, and mourned by none.

A Personal Extroduction from Text Number One

By ████████████

As I perused the eight hundred or so texts I had been given to choose from, this one seemed to jump out at me for a number of reasons. It was in many ways completely unlike the majority of *palmeresques* I had read, indeed in most respects it isn't really a *palmeresque* at all, and as such, is therefore both totally unrepresentative and yet uniquely interesting among the many more derivative and tedious pieces. A cursory search of the internet showed it to be represented on 687 independent web-pages (in June 2008), although some versions contained occasional noteworthy differences. In almost every case it was presented anonymously, as would be expected, however on three sites the author is named as P.H. Lovelace, clearly an unveiled reference to H.P. Lovecraft, the early 20th century English author best known for his ghost stories, and it does seem to be written in vague imitation of his style. The language itself is exaggeratedly old-fashioned and formal, as if attempting to emulate the language of a nineteenth-century English gentleman, which strongly suggests it was written by an American. Further to this, the detached formality of both the writing and the storyline itself makes it more than likely that the author was male.

What is most striking about the writing is its depiction of Amanda Palmer herself. The author has reinvented her very much in a Lovecraftian mould: she is cold, aloof, deluded, and most importantly, she is something of a failure in life. Basically in every sense the opposite of the Amanda I knew. And yet, somehow still quite likeable, like an embittered twin sister.

I am particularly intrigued by why the author might have decided upon this approach. It seems to me that there are three main likely interpretations. Firstly, that the writer, clearly a Lovecraft enthusiast, was uncomfortable with their own emotional reaction to Amanda's death, and thus took on both the style and detachment of Lovecraft as something of a mask to disguise their own emotional vulnerabilities, although in this context the last lines do come across as a little too cruel. Secondly, that the author, again a Lovecraft enthusiast, had no interest in Amanda or her works, and was motivated to write by having stumbled upon other examples of Palmeresque. To my mind this seems the most likely explanation, and if true, demonstrates that the appeal of the form has begun to reach beyond its original demographic. The third possibility is that the story had been written before Amanda's death, as a poor imitation of the works of Lovecraft, and was altered at a later date to fit the form. Personally I consider this to be the least likely explanation.

Whichever interpretation is settled upon, this story's tone and interpretation of Amanda tells a story in itself, and as such its very existence suggests much about the nature and breadth of the Palmeresque as it is currently evolving. And that is why I have chosen it.

* * * *

One last point: the names on the gravestones were all those of artists that had in some way or other worked with Amanda. Initially this was taken as sign that the author was familiar with Amanda's recordings and stage show, however it was later found that they were all amongst the *Artists I Support* section of her MySpace page at the time of her death, and therefore could easily have been found by anyone doing the slightest research.

One Day Last Week I Met Amanda Palmer

*A poem written upon the unexpected revelation that
Amanda Palmer was in fact the Devil Incarnate*

One day last week I saw Amanda Palmer
And yet six long months had passed since she had died
And though her visage bore the scars of all that time spent in the ground
Still I recognised Amanda in her eyes.

And I could tell she knew me too, for she was smiling
Or was it just the deathly grin of Fate?
And so I stood there, quite uncertain, and I pulled on my moustache
As she beckoned me to join her for something of a debate.

Well I wasn't going to turn down such an offer
For not often is one visited by the dead
So I made my way towards her, and I proffered her my hand
But she just laughed... "Don't you presume so much," she said

   "Oh I'm no longer that Amanda Palmer
   I've come here to reveal the Truth to You
   I am the very architect of all sorrows You endure
   I think you know me as the Devil, how do you do?!
   For often do I long to walk among you
   To join your eager reverie of despair

And from time to time I cast myself in lowly human form
That I might walk your streets and breathe your soiled air

Oh yes, I've worn a hundred thousand faces
My names have been too many to recall
But this Amanda Palmer, she was much more fun than most
I must admit, she will indeed prove memorable

But let me get to what must be an urgent question
Why am I here? Why have I come to talk to you?
Well I've been watching you young man, seen how you question
                                        everything
And thought I might pop up and offer you a clue...

Don't get me wrong, for this is not a friendly gesture
Oh no, I shall never be a friend to any Man
But your eagerness to know will sow the seeds of your destruction
So I thought I'd pop up and offer you a helping hand

For I've seen you out there looking for an honest soul
In a lying world where everyone's a whore
Well here I am, Your one and only honest soul, on a visit from
                                        the Damned
Your servant, and oh-so much more."

Well I was stumped and just a little bit bewildered
And though I tried, my tongue was tied, I couldn't speak
And Amanda just looked deep into my frightened little eyes, and she said
   "You don't believe in me yet young man! But you will! Now if you
   please, follow me!"

And with a bitter claw she grabbed my arm and dragged me
Far far away from all my company and friends,
   She said: "There's something I feel that I must show you, young man
   A kind of tour of all my children and their sins

"For you know, there IS a God that reigns above you
Though he is unconcerned with all your petty little games
And just between you and me, off the record, naturally,
The Bible is His word, just as it claims

"But Your God Above has long since lost all interest
And St Peter sits beside a rusty gate
And as he awaits his Lord's return he blames his loneliness on You,
I know, I've been up there, and taught him how to Hate.

"And before He left, Your Lord came down below for a visit
Said he was moving on to see more interesting things
He said to me "You were always my favourite Son,
You made it fun," and he smiled as he offered me his keys.

"Now at first I played the role with patient subtlety
Not realising quite why Your Lord had gone
But then I saw the seeds I'd sown, so very very long ago
Had taken root, and grown thick branches, and I realised I'd won.

"But let's go back, back to not long after the beginning
Let me show You how all these things have come to pass"
And with a gesture of her hand she banished every sign of Man
And I stood in a wilderness of trees and grass.

She said:
        "This is how it was soon after the beginning
And to start with it was such a simple deal
All this above was His, all that below our feet, was mine
And You guys dancing on the boundary with Your new-fangled Free
Will.

"Well, I wasn't interested in You at all to start with
Frankly, I just didn't give a damn
I was busy in the core, smelting down my metal ores
To build foundations for the realm I call a home

"And He seemed to be quite happy with His playthings
As You pranced about picking berries and hunting boar
But then I heard You come a-scratching on the roof of my foundations–
You were pilfering my precious metal ores

"So that was the first curse that I sent You
For You never realised that these things were mine
And no matter what You made, be it elegant or fierce
It would follow my intentions in good time

"Every broach became a beacon for my Vices
Each arrowhead a channel for my will
Attracting Pride and Envy, Greed and Lust and Wrath
Oh, so effortlessly was Your future sealed

"And up there on His throne He saw it coming
And I think He quite enjoyed the little game
For I heard Him laughing smugly as He tinkered with His toys
Inventing something new to help You on Your way

"And so He gave You Beauty, and the artfulness to catch it
And to free it from a block of wood, or stone
And, to be fair, You caught on quickly, with Your pigments and designs
And I could feel You slipping further from my realm

"So I pondered and considered and constructed
Until slowly I devised the perfect trap:
An elaborate concoction called Religion, in a hundred
Different drafts, scattered right across the map

"And every draft had its own unlikely stories
And every story had its heroes and its damned
And in Your tongue, I called Him God, And I called myself The Devil
But that was flattery on both counts, You understand.

"He gave You Faith, but I gave You Delusion
He gave You Love, but it was I who gave You Lust

He gave You untold riches in the next life, or so he said
But I gave You gold, and in gold You can immediately trust

"He gave You Contentment, but I gave You Glory
He gave You Restraint, but I gave You Desire
He gave You the quiet satisfaction of being one with Yourself
But I gave You Adventure, Invention, Ambition and Fear

"He gave You Music to seduce You from my passions
I gave You Writing to contain Your wildest fancies –
He turned my writing into poetry, I turned his Music into Dance
And so We pulled and pushed across the weary centuries

"So He and I, like spiteful playmates, spiked the potion
With ever more exotic complications
Until the mixture grew too rich to drink, too thick to pour
And bubbled mischievously with explosive implications

"Then We retreated, and We watched, and We waited
We had agreed there would be no more interference
For the scene had been well set, and the game was now afoot
And We gambled on the outcome with great impatience

"And how We smiled to see You tending to Your talents
Distilling many powerful notions from the mire
For the rest was up to You, and Your brilliance shining through
Would leave us gasping both in Awe and in Despair

"For it never was a game of Good and Evil
You could never draw its lines in Black and White
There were never simple choices; but a thousand different voices
Each one calling "Follow me" into the night

"And many of You led, and still more of You followed
And the thing that You call Culture soon evolved
But with Culture came Division, with Division came Derision
And so the story of Your Becoming slowly unfolds:

"Every temple was built upon the blood of cousins
Each palace was stained with greed's betrayal
And Your cities' bold foundations crushed the graves of many nations
As You congratulated Yourselves with vainglorious tales

"For War it was that begat Civilisation,
And Civilisation it was that begat War
And the two danced hand in hand across the Millennia,
Spreading Beauty and Disaster – ever demanding more

"And then there came those incredible Artworks
Far beyond even Our greatest conceptions:
There was Music that blended the compassion of a fool
With an arrogant man's bold assertions

"There were paintings that flooded the senses
Miraculous visions, exquisitely drawn
Almost painful to behold, they were so keenly seen
So desperately driven into form

"And so We marvelled at Your spirit, and We marvelled at Your Soul
And Your capacity to see beyond the Real
And yet the more You were surrounded by the spoils of your crimes
The more their dark foundations were concealed

"Creation and Destruction, Beauty and Death
To name the one is to define the other
Justice and Insanity, Holiness and Vanity
The parade of Hypocrites goes on forever"

And here she paused, as if lost upon reflection
Of the most dramatic import of her words
And with a gesture of her wrist she beckoned in the mist
And I was swallowed in its billowing twists and turns

But then, suddenly I saw it was a thousand million ghosts
A seething mass of limbs all writhing and straining

As if a parody of carnival grotesques had gone berserk –
For She was showing me the Hypocrites parading

And so I watched as many centuries of denial drifted past
Until finally she spoke: "Please forgive my visual gimmickry
I know there is no need to impress you with such tricks
But I offer you these scenes in casual sincerity

"For Your curse, the curse of Man, is that You seek to understand
But the closer that You look the less You see
And whilst You're staring at a pin-head, searching out the Soul of Man
A whole world of unimagined answers passes by

"Oh it's all a matter of perspective, you understand
You cannot see what you're looking at without looking away
And these tormented Souls that drift, forever cursing their desires
Deny themselves a life, for fear of losing face

"These are not the spirits of the dead or damned
They are the everyday folk of your modern land
Alive, but not alight, they pass the time

"And then at night their dreams are filled
With every fear and taboo thrill
Before they wake, and once again they stand in line

"And then this quiet dissatisfaction
Slowly eats away inside them
Until they wake one day to find their heart is hollow

"And all that they can feel
Is resentment and betrayal
Though towards whom and by what they do not know

"And soon they are condemning
And soon they are a-preaching
And banging fists on doors for to complain

"But what they really crave
Is far too dangerous to know -
They've given up, and always look the other way

"For the most devastating Silence is of words left unspoken
Of fantasies hounded by shame -
For they wither the Soul 'till the Spirit is broken
Or explode into ugly disdain

"Sure, Truth is Beauty, and Beauty is Truth
But so is Violence, Corruption and Fear
So make sure you look up when you're walking on water
But look down when you're crossing the mire

"Every man, every woman and child is born
With a Vision that is waiting to sing
But for most it is easier to simply deny
There is anything burning within

"For to sing would bring Confusion, and Confusion courts Despair
And so the scaffolding around them tumbles down
And so for fear of being left up in the air, their eyes are closed
And their mouths will ne'er conceive a melodious sound

"I look into Your cities' sallow eyes in search of light
And certainly activity bewilders –
I see a veritable hive of imperfections, masturbations
Titillations, and distractions to consider

"So I seek beneath the glamour and monotonous clamour
For the heretics, the martyrs, the condemned
And I call upon the glorious hole-builders of old
Those champions on whom I could always depend

"But nobody answers, nobody comes forth
No, not one whisper of a creeping revelation
Not the slightest stink of chaos, nor the briefest glimpse of Love
Beyond the usual smug self-satisfaction

"Oh, where are the true Saints and the true Sinners?
Your visions have become more tedious than Your crimes
And whilst You measure Your reflection in the mirror of Deception
Every one of You betrays the next in line

"So if you are truly searching for an honest soul
Waste not your idle time splitting day from night
It is right here among the Damned that will you find that steady hand
For only in the Darkness shines the Light

"Only the chained Soul cries out for freedom
Only the muddied heart looks up toward the sky above
And there is not one living Soul among your many brethren
That is not Damned by his own hand for want of Love

"For that is why I made Amanda Palmer
Why I chose to come among you in her form
For the spirit of a singer can reach deep into the heart
Of every coward and deceiver ever born

"Oh yes, Music is the king of all emotions
It rules them with a firm and steady hand
Demanding silence of the ego's bold commotions
It stills the rampant miseries of the Damned

"And what better way to wreak my merry havoc
Than to fill Your wanton worn out Spirits with desire
For a voice that reaches forth with such exquisite sexual drama
And a beauteous form, richly wrought from sexual fire

"Yes that is why I made Amanda Palmer
To light up the flame of hope within your dreams
For without it You become as tedious as the Bible can seem long
When it is lit, You entertain with some adequacy

"Oh yes, that is why I made Amanda Palmer
For to remind You what it is to be alive

For it is hope defines despair, and success longs for disaster
And in those vices my idle fingers thrive"

And with those words she vanished in an instant
And I was back among the gardens with my friends
And though the perfumes smelt so sweet
And the fellowship seemed complete
I was alone, for Innocence had found its End!

A Personal Extroduction from Text Number Three

By ████████

Well, where do I begin? For a start this poem doesn't really fit any of the pre-requisites for a *palmeresque* and yet I found it both fascinating and perplexing in equal measure, and on so many levels, not all of them good. To my mind it is clearly attempting to take on the tradition of the metaphysical poets of old. I see the shades of Coleridge, Blake, Donne, Milton, all looming over it and most probably looking down disapprovingly. Don't get me wrong, this is not a great poem by any means, but it certainly tries, occasionally almost gets there, then comes out with a line so clumsy and naive that these aspirations are quickly forgotten. Indeed I occasionally found myself laughing out loud, a rare event indeed, particularly when judging literary competitions.

Let me start with the presentation of Amanda Palmer herself. By casting her as a literal face of the Devil the author has effectively deified her, remaking in the guise of a magical being. This is perhaps not so surprising given the fan based nature of the origins of the Palmeresque. But then, as the story (if that is the right word) unfolds the magic is somewhat tarnished by her general sense of dissatisfaction. (I imagine that is why she felt the need to return to our realm and report on the problem, as this is not revealed in the text.) Towards the end the Devil explains that she made herself into Amanda Palmer basically to stir things up a little as she was bored. Not a glorious spiritual conclusion really. Thus on the narrative level this poem therefore fails, but it does retain some dignity through its commitment to its argument.

As for the psycho-spiritual debate that forms the main body of the text, well it is hard to know whether it reveals a complex many angled psychological argument, or a series of simplistic and contradictory truisms, most likely the latter. Certainly there are some stanzas that are rich in pretentions of beauty and profundity, some even feel quotable, and yet the overall argument is more than a little incoherent, and inconclusive. If I had any faith that this was in fact the author's intention, that being to imply the complex and contradictory nature of the human psyche as understood today, then I would take off my hat and introduce the world to a fine new poet, but alas, I have no such faith, and suspect that this is merely the product of "woolly thinking". It is, however, these many contradictions that both fascinate and perplex me. I simply don't quite understand what the author is trying to do, and suspect that he (I am fairly certain it was written by a man) doesn't either.

Nonetheless it is certainly not without talent, technique and ability, not to mention a distinct flair for words. I particular enjoyed the mixing of old formal English with more modern terms.

Generally I have a fundamental problem with most modern poetry; indeed I have in my time been called reactionary. But I find that almost every example I read is toying with nothing more than the mundane details of modern middle class ennui. Of course there are exceptions, but where are the big issues? Where is the search for the eternal? Where is the responsibility of the artist to delve deeper than his fellow man (woman)? And also, I have issues with the discarding of form. It seems to me that much modern poetry is really prose unnaturally divided up into lines, with no more sense of rhythm than a traffic jam. What strikes me most about this text is that it attempts all these things: the discipline of regular rhythm and rhyme; the search for the eternal; delving into the big issues. And though it frequently fails at everything it strives towards, every box is at least ticked.

I therefore must wholeheartedly applaud the intentions of the author, whilst sighing woefully (and occasionally laughing uproariously) at the obvious failings of the text itself. I only hope he/she learns to focus his/her thoughts more coherently in future works.

On the Near Perfect Death of Amanda Palmer

It is a widely held notion that at the moment of death one's whole
life flashes before one, and indeed that is almost always the case. So
as Amanda Palmer lay dying she was surprised to find someone
else's life flashing before her. Or rather she would have been surprised had she had the consciousness to question it. As it was she
just lay there, drifting upon the dreamlike images that passed
through her mind, images that seemed strangely unfamiliar, and yet
somehow comforting. In the distance she could hear herself gasping
for air, feel the blood leaving her body, taking with it what little
strength remained, but all that seemed like a memory now, of little
concern. She had no idea how this had happened. Nor did it seem
to matter: this was the first time she had died, and she was keen to
see what the experience had to offer. Even in this situation she considered herself an Artist, and is it not an artist's job to explore the
extremities of experience? If she was to die, then she would do it
properly. In life she had always prided herself on her courage to
leap into the abyss, and there was no reason to feel differently now.
This was just another challenge. To cling to life when the ultimate
culmination of experience lay within her grasp would be a betrayal
of everything she had claimed to be, everything she had dreamt she
was. Certainly she had had her moments of doubt. There had been
times, many times, when the fear of finding she was ordinary had

eaten away at her confidence, made her question if she had it in her. But this was her chance, her final and most glorious chance to prove herself, to be the bold explorer, to map the very borders of existence, and she was determined not to find herself wanting.

But none of that explained the life that seemed to be flashing before her, which was definitely not hers, not that she recognised anyway, and that was the puzzle. "Well that's a bit fucking weird," she thought, wrestling what remained of her consciousness from the corporeal remains below. Was it below? Already she realised she was making assumptions. Open-mindedness. In situations like this that was the key. No assumptions, no rushed explanations, just sit back and enjoy the ride—she didn't really mean that last bit but felt the need to state it to herself regardless. Why did she do that? She always did that. She had after all considered "Miss Placed Bravura" as a potential stage name some years earlier. No, come on girl, focus on what's happening. This is a one-time shot. And with not inconsiderable effort she slowly managed to bring the vision into clearer focus. Whoever's life it was she was seeing, or rather visiting, for that was closer to how it felt, they were by now considerably older than her, and seemed to have given themselves over to the domestic simplicities of motherhood. "How fucking tedious was that!" she thought, as the envisioned life drew towards it's close until suddenly it blinked into nothing leaving her with a slightly uncomfortable feeling of grand-maternal love and domestic self-satisfaction, which she tried to form into words, to expel them aloud from her gut, but all that came out was a long and garbled "*fuuuuuccck!!!*"

Okay, so this was nothing, nothingness, she got that. What now. Isn't she supposed to flicker out of existence, or move on to a higher plane or something? And hey, what about the white light? Shouldn't there be a white light? . . . The nothing continued being nothing. If she was to be entirely honest, and really there was little point in anything else at this stage, she would have to admit that this "nothing" business was beginning to freak her out a little. Indeed the notion of eternal nothingness was becoming ever-more feasible, and she didn't like that thought at all. She sat down. Well at least there was a floor, so "nothing" might be too strong a word. Slightly . . . But nonetheless . . . The unease was slowly turning to mild panic. *Now girl, get a grip of yourself*, she thought, *this is no time for panicking . . . No time for panicking!? Surely if ever there were a time for panicking this was it. And didn't she have all the time in the world, beyond the world. Might as well get the panic over and done with so she can settle in and relax.* So she stood up and screamed, screamed with all her considerable might sending an echo around the emptiness that lasted a good few seconds. *Aha. An echo means walls . . . and walls often mean a door? All I have to do is keep walking straight . . . and in time . . .* At this point she hit something solid with her head. *Fuck! That hurt.* Almost immediately a door appeared where she had hit her head. It was a large panelled door, freshly painted in black gloss with an enormous brass knob at chest height and a rather splendid engraved brass letterbox which she proceeded to bellow through. *Helllooooo!* . . . Nothing. She was just about to shout again when she thought she caught the distant tapping a footsteps on a hard stone floor. Yes, definitely coming her way, and in something of a rush. She pressed her ear to the door. As the footsteps got closer she could just hear an intermittent wheezing accompanying them. Suddenly they slowed, then stopped.

After a moment's pause the door clunked quietly to itself and then swung open with a self-satisfied sigh. Stood before her was a tall, slim, elegant, red-faced gentleman, dressed in English tweeds and wearing a fine waxed moustache and a somewhat apologetic expression.

"I am so sorry, Miss Palmer. So sorry for my lateness," he wheezed, clearly still catching his breath.

"Such tardiness is unforgivable. And on today of all days."

He beckoned her to come inside. She stepped through the door into what seemed to be the exact same nothing of the previous room, if room is even the right word for an undefined space filled with nothing.

"This way Miss Palmer. Please follow me . . . follow me. Just along here . . . this way." He seemed to be urgently hurrying her along, and though she dutifully followed she was beginning to have second thoughts. "Come along now, we're already running late. . ." At this she stopped.

"Late for what? . . . And what is all this anyway? . . . Where am I? . . . Where are we going? . . . At least that is what she thought she said. What actually came out was somewhat more garbled and shot through with expletives. But either way, the moustachioed gentleman was entirely unfazed.

"No time for questions, Miss Palmer. Not now. They'll be plenty later. Just come along please." Although this entire situation was more than a little peculiar, it struck her as particularly odd that every now and again he would stop, look searchingly left and right into the absent cavern of nothing, and then purposefully turn one direction or another and stride forward, checking his watch and muttering to himself before calling back to hurry her on.

"Nearly there now," he said, turning again, this time to the right, and glancing at his watch. A hundred or so yards later he stopped.

"Et voila!" He gestured smugly towards . . .

"A ladder! You've got to be fucking kidding me!"

"I kid you not, Miss Palmer. After all, when has getting somewhere important ever been easy? Please follow me . . . and don't get too far behind, we're already late." And before she could say another word he was disappearing up the ladder, calling back from time to time to hurry her along.

She must have climbed a good hundred yards or so when the ladder abruptly came to an end. Abruptly, as there was no indication of its impending conclusion - it seemed to be propped up against nothing at all. It wasn't until she reached the very top that she realised that it was in fact leaning against what can only be described as a hole in the side of the nothing, or rather a tunnel, shaped something like a gothic arch and with brightly painted external baroque finishings. She peered hesitantly inside only to hear her moustachioed companion calling her along into the dark and surprisingly damp interior. It was barely tall enough to crouch in, so she had to go on all fours. The walls seemed to be made of bricks, old crumbling bricks at that, and were lined with a good century worth of slime and moss and... well, she didn't even want to know what that was.

She must have been in the tunnel for a few minutes when a dim light began to glow somewhere in the distance, marking, or so she hoped, the other end. *Is this my bright light?* she thought, slightly mocking herself. *My loved ones waiting to greet me at the end of some damp fucking hole!* "Wait-up!" she called into the dim but ever-brightening distance, and made what effort she could to speed her progress.

At the other end the passage seemed to contract somewhat before opening out into an obviously bigger and brighter space. As she clambered through she realised she was climbing up out of the rather grand fireplace of what can only be described as a Queen Anne drawing room, fully bedecked with richly textured fabrics and tassels, still lifes on the wall. She collapsed on a surprisingly comfortable armchair to get her breath back.

"We really must hurry along you know, we're late as it is," said the moustachioed gentleman tapping at his watch before opening the French windows to reveal a most unexpected view: they were looking out at the most unimaginably enormous furniture warehouse, filled to the very top with a towering chaos of chairs stacked upon tables stacked upon desks, upon wardrobes, upon barrels, upon chests upon... were those coffins?

"You gotta be kidding me!" At the top right-hand corner from their perspective she could see door with the word EXIT writ large in chalk above. "We gotta climb up there?"

"It'll be a piece of cake, Miss Palmer, with cherries on top, if you catch my drift. Just follow along closely. I know the way." And with that he was gone. Amanda remained seated. A few moments later his head reappeared around the open door, his eyebrows raised. She paused for dramatic purpose.

"You know, I think I might just sit here for a minute. I'm guessing you can't make me move, or you wouldn't be bothering with all that polite cajoling."

"Come now, Miss Palmer, that won't do, really won't do at all . . ."

"Well I'm not budging, not until you answer some questions." She leant forward, and gesticulated. "I mean, what the hell is this. Is this Hell!? It's a fucking furniture warehouse. That's what it is! Is Hell a fucking furniture warehouse? Is that what you're telling me?"

"More of a dispatch depot really."

"Ok, so it's a fucking dispatch depot. What the fuck am I doing here? And why the fuck do I have to climb the fucking thing!? And... and... what the fucking hell is going on?!" She felt surprisingly refreshed after that little rant.

"Please, do calm down my dear."

"Don't you fucking patronise me."

"Sincere apologies, Miss Palmer. I understand that this might seem somewhat perplexing. We are indeed moving via unconventional routes. But this is an unconventional circumstance. There is no precedent, no accommodations made for such a happening. It truly is most irregular, so please do come along, we really don't want to make things any worse." And with that he was gone again.

"Worse for who?" She said this to herself as she didn't really want an answer. Reluctantly she stood up and moved to the doorway to address the situation of the climb.

"But why furniture?" she called after him.

"Everyone needs furniture. Quite a sound investment I would say."

The ascent proved far easier than she had imagined, like being a small child again, climbing Furniture Castle on moving-in day. And as she reached the top, a good 200 feet up, she surprised herself by yelling aloud "BoooooHa!" If she didn't know better she might have mistaken that for a shout of glee. Truth be told, and slime aside, she was beginning to quite enjoy this little run-around, although when she noticed the moustachioed gentleman looking at her through the doorway she quickly changed her expression to one of mere tolerance.

"This way please." he said, gesturing inside with the smallest hint of a knowing smile. And he was gone again.

"So what's next?" she thought, this time ready for anything. As she passed through the doorway into what seemed to be a Boston back alley, complete with its associated stink of rotting food and piss, she couldn't help but mouth the words "curiouser and curiouser."

"It is indeed a shame that we have to arrive by the stage door —we had such an entrance planned for you . . . dancing girls, magicians, acrobats, midgets . . . the whole damn works. But then under the circumstances . . . well, it just doesn't seem quite appropriate now . . ."

They reached the stage door, clearly defined as such by the elderly security guard, and the flickering sign above saying *Stage Door* in pink and green neon. As he opened the door the guard acknowledged them with a polite "Good evening Sir, Ma'am."

Inside, the main corridor was lined with a veritable menagerie of circus performers, burlesque girls and street entertainers, the majority in a not inconsiderable state of undress. Midgets in blue spandex hotpants abounded, many stood upon each others' shoulders in small groups. There were dancing girls galore, dressed (or becoming dressed) entirely in feathers of innumerable different but equally bright colours. There were clowns of every shape, size and demeanour; magicians in top hat and tails with enormous handlebar moustaches; a plethora of stilt-walkers, each strumming quietly to themselves upon a ukulele, mouthing the words of some inaudible song, whilst stooping somewhat so as to avoid banging their heads on the ceiling. As they slowly elbowed their way through the general hubbub and melee of bodies they occasionally passed an open dressing room door, each revealing a more surprising scene than the last. A gathering of great philosophers, at least men in false beards and wigs dressed as great philosophers: she recognised Socrates, Schopenhauer, Blake, and Newton, but who was that young man in a tuxedo? Perhaps Wittgenstein? The next open door revealed a girl in a dress made entirely from pages of *Moby Dick* – she wasn't sure how she knew it was *Moby Dick*, but of that fact she was certain. At the girl's feet was an elderly gentleman, on his knees, attempting to look up her skirt with his hand-held spectacles whilst she danced about in a mildly provocative manner. A few doors later opened onto a blazing row taking place between a dandy-highwayman and a lady grandfather clock. And so it went on, corridor after corridor, turning after turning until they came to some stairs.

Just as they were about to ascend, a rounded and slightly oafish gentleman, in a superbly huge top hat and bright red tailcoat (presumably a circus ringmaster of sorts) came bustling down the stairs, pushing and shoving his way through the crowd whilst shouting through a megaphone "More delays, more delays . . . please remain in place and await further instruction . . . more delays, more delays . . ." nearly deafening Amanda as he passed. At this her moustachioed friend immediately seized the moment, diving headlong into the wake of the oversized gentleman calling out "Make way for Miss Palmer . . . make way for Miss Palmer . . ." whilst dragging Amanda behind him by the hand. This seemed to work as they were on the stairs in no time, though she did notice many accusatory glances cast in her direction. As they made their way up the stairs the crowd thinned considerably until by the third flight there was only one solitary midget-acrobat carefully applying gold makeup to his legs and torso. He looked up at them as they passed:

"You better be good. He's in a foul mood today," he said before returning his attention to the gilding of his nipple.

"What the fuck does that mean?" Amanda asked with some urgency as soon as they were out of earshot.

"Oh, nothing for you to be concerned about Miss Palmer. Internal politics, nothing more. Come along now. We're nearly there."

They were by now stood at the top of the stairs, before a set of rich red velvet curtains that hid a large double swing door.

"What's the show anyways?"

"It's a musical drama loosely based upon Dante's *Inferno*. Such a shame . . . you would have loved it . . . great set pieces . . . Paul McCartney dragging behind him for all eternity the great weight of every unnecessary sentimental refrain that ever flowed from his pen... and a grinning Kurt Cobain who giggles when you tickle him... it was such fun..."

"Wait a minute, McCartney's not dead,"

"Indeed he isn't. And yet the depth of sentimentality must weigh heavy on his shoulders every day..."

His face was partially lit by a sign that stated *Quiet Please* above the curtain door, and as he spoke Amanda noticed that something was, well, slipping a little.

"Is that even real?"

"What do you mean Miss Palmer?"

"That moustache. Is it real? It seems to have . . . moved."

"Why it is absolutely real. A 100% genuine finest handmade moustache by Dinsley & Sons, theatrical suppliers to Her Majesty the Queen. I assure you it is the envy of many here today."

"What does the Queen need false moustaches for?"

"Some questions are best left un-asked Miss Palmer. This way please . . . after you . . ." and he parted the curtain and opened the door, gesturing for her to go through first.

She was momentarily perplexed by this moustache situation – why would someone wear a false moustache in the afterlife? - and thus paid little attention to where they were going. That is until the applause began, which caught her so much by surprise that she swung round violently, almost losing her footing, just in time to see the lights go on. They were walking across a stage. The spotlights were on them, or rather her, and, judging by the sound, it was a full house. The crowd was uproarious at the sight of her, but she didn't know what she was expected to do. Of course, crowds didn't scare her, she fully retained her self-possession and was about to do her notionally-patented-punk-curtsy when she felt the falsely-moustachioed man's hand gently taking her wrist.

"Come along now, Miss Palmer, we're nearly there. Let's not get distracted . . . And mind how you tread."

The applause slowly petered out as the audience began to realise this was not the start of the show, and, before she could regain her composure, they were off the stage and heading down another corridor. They came to a large mahogany door, stoically ornamented with a small brass plaque clearly stating *Theatre Manager*.

"Et voila. We are here. And this, I am afraid, is where I must leave you, Miss Palmer. I do hope you enjoyed the little journey . . . Just knock and enter. You are expected." He turned to leave. Before she could think of anything to say he added "Don't let him bully you now . . . oh, and break a leg, so to speak." And he was gone.

"So," she thought, "what next . . ." and was just contemplating whether to go right ahead and knock, or perhaps take a minute to digest what was going on, feeling something like a naughty schoolgirl outside the headmaster's office, when a voice seemed to boom through the door:

"Miss Palmer, please come in." It was a strong voice, vigorous and commanding, though this was undermined somewhat by the distinct and clearly faked German accent.

The door opened onto an undistinguished room, much as you might expect of a theatre manager's office. There were old wooden filing cabinets, a large oak desk, a few chairs upholstered in leather, and the walls were predictably lined with bookcases, each considerably overfilled not just with books but also ornaments, props and various loose papers. But it was the man stood behind the desk that immediately caught her attention, or rather his extraordinarily oversized moustache.

"You're not fucking Nietzsche!"

* * * *

"Indeed, Ich bin nicht more Herr Nietzsche zan yung Hardy who brought du hier ist ein Englischer gentleman. But it seems to micht zat die question du bist really asking ist more 'Is all zis eine product of your own imagination or is it *real*?' by vich du no doubt mean 'is zehr some external independent influence involved in zese things?' Vell, Ich bin nicht really at liberty to answer such direct questions, but, and zis ist strictly off ze record, let us just say zat vee supply die substance, and zat you supply die vindow dressing. Alzough naturalicht any answer I give ist necessarily no answer at all."

"Okay . . . so you're some sort of male authority figure that I am perceiving as Nietzsche."

"Zat's zie idea, zough Ich bin really more of ein psychological evaluator. And I must say it is interesting zat du habe chosen to project me as Herr Nietzsche. Most people go for Freud, or Jesus, or zeir mutter . . . Ich had Oprah recently. Haven't had Nietzsche for quite some time . . . Of course I only verk in die Vestern vorld. I'm sure it gets a whole lot veirder die further east you go." By now his accent was distinctly slipping, and causing him some difficulty. "Look, do you mind if I drop the voice?" he said in a more middle class, but equally fake, nasal New York tone.

"No, no, absolutely, feel free."

"And to answer your other un-asked question, that being "what is it with all the moustaches?" Well it seems moustaches, and particularly false moustaches, have played a pivotal role in your life, hence their predominance here." And with that he began to stroke the enormous bush of a moustache that bedecked his upper lip as if to demonstrate the point until suddenly and somewhat dramatically he banged both hands on the desk.

"So! . . . Please, Amanda, might I call you Amanda? Please, do sit down. I imagine you probably have some questions."

"Well, yes, I probably do . . ." She paused for a moment. "I died. I get that. I guess I was kinda expecting the whole shebang. You know, life flashing before me, bright light, family there to greet me... And what do I get?" Her voice rose a little in both volume and pitch. "Someone else's life! Someone who seemed to get unimaginably old and a whole bunch of grand-maternal pride thrown in for good measure! A camp Englishman in a false moustache taking me on what can only be described as a run-around! And now my head is being "evaluated" by Nietzsche, or should I say a man wearing an absurd moustache who can't keep up a German accent for more than a few sentences! So yes, I have some fucking questions! Like . . . what the fuck is going on?!"

"Hmmm, you didn't get it then . . . the "run-around" . . . shame . . . I know Hardy put quite a bit of effort into it. Still! Limited by circumstance I guess. And what a circumstance! Most unusual. Even unprecedented, in my time anyway."

Amanda leant forward. "Listen. Is there anything at stake here? I mean, are there consequences? You said "evaluator." What I mean is . . ."

Leaning back on his chair so as to keep the distance uniform: "You mean am I evaluating you now? No, it's nothing like that. My job is more to help you evaluate yourself. So no consequences, permission to speak freely and all that."

"Okay so spill it then. What *is* going on?"

"Right . . . So . . . Yes . . . Well, there has been something of what you might call a clerical error. Just a minor one, but regrettably there have been repercussions . . . Particularly for you . . . and for another Amanda Palmer, of Wilmington, Ontario, come to that . . ."

". . . What do you mean clerical error? And repercussions?"

He raised his finger as if to command silence. "I'll cut to the chase, so to speak. You see we were expecting you both, and at almost the same time, on the scale of things that is. And we had a great show planned for each of you. But then, what with her enthusiasm to get here, and your reluctance . . . well, you see, you arrived in the wrong order. She got your life and you got hers . . ."

Amanda was understandably baffled by this.

"This has never happened before I assure you . . . Now, of course, we put everything on hold as soon as we realised. But unfortunately these things can't be recycled. Which leaves us with something of a problem, that being: what do we do with you now?" He noticed a distinct look of concern pass across Amanda's face at this and so added ". . . to amend the situation that is."

"You mean you've screwed up my death?"

"Well not the Death itself, that was conducted admirably by all . . . more the processing thereof. But fear thee not. There's always a way around such things. We've just got to find it. Well, actually there *are* a great many potential ways around *this*. But I have always prided myself on being fair. And I feel it is only fair that you should be given a say in the matter. That's off the record, naturally . . . And after all, I am the Big Boss here, head of department, senior management so to speak . . ."

"Okay . . . ?"

"You really didn't get it then . . . Hardy's little show . . . it didn't feel . . ." here his words hung in the air, a little like a question but with additional hope, ". . . symbolically significant, in any way? . . . Hmmm, shame. Still I'm not at all surprised. It was clutching somewhat at straws."

"What was I supposed to get?"

"*Supposed* is really too strong a word. *Hoped* or *encouraged* might be more on target. Well you see normally . . . hmmm . . . How can I explain . . . errrm . . . The way it works is this. A client, or rather a person, passes over, right? Now obviously that can be quite a jarring experience. I mean one minute they're running a bath, or tickling a small child, or heading to the corner store with every intention of buying 35 cherry-candy-shoelaces, (that was my last case), and the next, poof, its all over, they've *run down the curtain and joined the choir-invisible.*" He seemed quite proud of this quotation, even attempting an almost recognisable English accent, adding under his breath "Accents were never really my thing."

"Anyway, that's where the whole *life flashing before you* thing comes in. It's in many ways the completion. Or conclusion. No, more completion really. *Comfort's balm for the yearning Soul,* as we like to say. The victim . . . errrm, person, who has passed that is . . . is presented with a kind of recapitulation, all freshly prepared here by us: to relive in an instant their entire contribution, to see it as a whole, complete and perfect in its entirety. We tie up all the loose ends so to speak. And once our work is done all that remains is a carefully crafted sense of self-satisfaction at a life well lived, and they are ready for the next level. Forgive me if I am not being entirely clear here. These things are not well suited to expression through words, as with all the finer things in life . . . or death come to that."

"I think I'm getting it."

"And, you see, that's the point. We're supposed to be invisible: stage hands in the final drama; the unseen mechanics who work the illusion. And, well, it all seems to have gone a bit tits-up this evening. Now here you are talking to me! Unprecedented! Really . . . And as for Mrs. Palmer . . . that doesn't even bear consideration . . . And that's what Hardy's little show was all about. We were kind of hoping it would all just click for you. A little optimistic I know. But needs must where the Devil spits, so to speak."

"Hardy's little show?"

"Yes, what you called the *run-around*. The intention was to somehow show you your life, and bring you that contented feeling of completion through the subtle art of metaphor. Hardy's idea, he always was a poet at heart, though admittedly not a very good one. And the truth is he had very little to work with, and at such short notice too . . . You might want to thank him later by the way. It was somewhat beyond the call of duty."

"Ok, you *have* lost me now."

"Let me talk you through it." He began rummaging through the contents of a desk drawer, then triumphantly looked up, waving a piece of paper covered in handwritten notes and diagrams. "Here we are . . ." and he took a moment to look over both sides of the paper.

"Right. In brief: It started with nothing, emptiness, a blank slate waiting to be filled. Then a door, a way through, you begin to find your direction, your purpose. And then you come upon a ladder, a way up, a shortcut to finding your place in the world. Although of course this has to lead to a long dark tunnel, for there is no achievement or reward without effort. Not in that life anyway. But you struggle on, determined to see it through to the end. And lo, you rise from the ashes, being the fireplace, into the full glory of civilisation, as symbolised by that rather fine Queen Anne drawing room, with particularly comfortable armchairs . . . it says here that you noticed that feature . . . Now many folks might have stopped there, with all the comforts of civilisation to satisfy them. But not you. Not Amanda Palmer. Oh no. You have to create a mountain, you need to climb still further . . . though just why that was symbolised by towering piles of furniture I am not entirely sure—I guess we had a lot of it available—and so you make your the way to the very top. Now, that takes you backstage at a show of your own devising, and yet you are still uncertain as to what the show is really about, and the applause you receive feels, to you anyway, unjustified. You are honoured but not truly understood, even by yourself, that is until you arrive here, in my office." He puts the paper down on his desk. "And there you have it! . . . your life revealed in all its many completenesses . . . Of course being a metaphor it works on many other levels. I mean think about it. Is that not the way a song comes into the world? Or a perfect description the evolution of most human relationships? Does it not outline the very spirit of Adventure, of Passion, of the whole Human Experience? And therein lies the perfection of your completeness . . . I guess that didn't quite come across . . . indeed the usefulness of metaphors can be limited at moments of great import."

Amanda wasn't sure quite how she was expected to react at this point, but had the distinct impression she was being given the hard sell. "So . . . ?" This was more of an encouragement for him to continue than a statement.

"Well, you see, that is the beauty of it. Your life was an expression of your Art, and your Art an expression of your life, the two perfectly in balance, one journey writ both large and small, with too many symmetries to even consider. To continue beyond the moment of your demise would have sent the whole grand edifice toppling. And really that wouldn't do now would it?"

". . . Guess not."

"So you're happy then. You get it."

"I guess."

"And you feel completion. You're ready to move on . . . to the next level . . ."

"Well . . . I . . . no, wait. Do I have a choice then?"

"Well, in theory I suppose you do. But would that not be a tremendous aesthetic error? I mean, consider the legacy, your legacy. What you have worked towards all your life. You are on a cusp here my dear." Amanda winced inwardly at the *dear* word, but considered what was being said too important to interrupt. "On one side there is Jim Morrison, on the other, Iggy Pop. Keith Moon or Ringo Star. Buddy Holly or Cliff Richard. Brian Jones or Ronnie Wood. I could go on. You have earned the chance to become a legend. Of course, no one can guarantee what will actually occur. But the chance is there, and really should not be wasted. To die with the eyes of the world upon you is a glorious thing indeed. And there is also the death itself to consider. Why it was perfect. The timing, the means, the execution . . . You will remain forever at your peak, the pinnacle, your very greatest of moments. Your fans will most likely canonise you. *Here lies Amanda Palmer, she lived and died for her Art.*"

"And how exactly did I die? I mean, what happened?"

"You don't remember? Oh no, of course you don't . . . but that's not really the point. The point is . . ."

"No really, I'd like to know. I remember . . . there was blood . . . no, it's gone."

"To be honest we don't actually have that information to hand. But I bet it was a good'un. It had to be good, what with the show they laid on for you . . . were planning to lay on that is, before this little problem occurred. I haven't seen so many midgets in years. Not all in the same place anyways. And their rendition of the Siege of Leningrad, well that was . . . genius. Sheer genius. I laughed until it hurt!"

"Ok, Stop! So let me get this straight. I died, by some undisclosed manner probably involving a lot of blood. Somehow you seem to have misplaced my life, or rather given it to someone else, and now, through a series of crude metaphors you are trying to convince me that dying was the right thing to do. Am I in the ballpark?"

"Well, basically, yes. I suppose you could put it that way. But would it not be better and more appropriate to see this whole experience as a kind of post-punk expression of mortality?"

"Fuck that! What I am getting at here is: why are you trying to convince me? I mean, why does it matter what I think? Surely you can just send me wherever it is I am to go, regardless. Unless . . ."

"Come now, Miss Palmer. A wise soul knows when the time has come to die. Only a fool would choose to linger on whilst all their life's attainments turn to dust about them."

"Now I know you're spouting bullshit. What is that? Some kind of self-help guide for the recently deceased? I would have thought the time for platitudes was over now . . . and by the way, your moustache is slipping."

He pressed the excessively large squirrel of a moustache back into place.

"Please, Miss Palmer, don't rush to judgement here. It is my job to ensure your . . . how can I put this . . . let's say cleansing of the grime of life before you continue onwards. And as I said, that normally is a simple, almost automated process. But here I am having to do it by hand, so to speak. So please do bear with me. This isn't easy you know. And consider for a moment poor Mrs. Palmer. How do you think she feels? Having led a polite and God-fearing life to the age of 92 she now finds that she is a risqué performance artist who parades about in stripy stockings. The revelation almost gave her a heart attack—that is had she not already died of one. So please, stop thinking only of yourself. Consider the rest of us."

"Excuse me! *I'm* the one whose death has been cocked up by some administrative error. I think I have every right to be pissed!"

"I suppose you do. Anyway . . . where were we . . ."

"And what happens if I refuse? If I don't play ball. What if I like the *grime of life* and don't wish to be parted from it?"

"Well really that would be most unconventional of you, not to mention unfortunate."

"For who exactly? For me? Or for you?"

At this he paused. He could see this was going to be difficult and wasn't at all certain how to proceed.

"Miss Palmer. I am not trying to trick you, or manipulate you. I am only trying to clear up a little messy situation that by all rights should not have occurred. I accept full responsibility for my part. Can you say the same?"

"So far as I can see your little mess has fuck all to do with me."

"Ah, well, you may say that, but honestly, had you not clung to life with such tenacity then none of this would have happened."

"Listen, mate. You can't shovel your shit onto me. Anyway, you haven't answered my question. What if I refuse to be *completed*?"

"I sincerely hope it doesn't come to that. But I suppose, if that were to be the outcome, you would be deemed not ready."

"And . . . ? What would that mean?"

"Well I guess there are two possible options. Either you could stay here and help us with our work, or . . ."

"Or what?"

"Or you could go back until you are deemed ready."

"Go back? . . . you mean . . . back to being alive?"

"Yes, that would be the other option. But really, it is most inadvisable. I mean, consider the aesthetics, the Art. It would all be most horribly undermined. And there may be unforeseen repercussions. Things could get . . . complicated."

"Fuck aesthetics! Fuck complicated! I choose to live."

"Really, Miss Palmer, that is a most undesirable position to take." Here his tone changed, becoming darker and a little threatening. "Listen! Let me ask you: do you really think it will last? The success, the glory, the adoration, the eyes of the world upon you? Oh no. It will fade. You'll see. Like plucked flowers in an empty vase it will wither and die before your very eyes. And, knowing what you know now, you will everyday curse your decision to return."

"No, you listen, Herr Nietzsche, or whatever your name is. This is your fuck up not mine. There is no fucking way I am staying here, and by your own admission I am not ready to *move on* whatever that means. So fucking send me back!"

"As you wish, Miss Palmer, as you wish. But don't say I didn't warn you."

His words were becoming more distant, echoing around her head like church bells in a bowl of water.

"You'll be seeing me again, Miss Palmer, and sooner than you may think!"

Now the whole room seemed to be retreating. She felt something akin to being sucked up into a syringe and then squirted out with great force. Then darkness, nothing but darkness, and the faintest distant bleeping of what sounded like . . .

hospital machinery.

* * * *

Amanda had no way of knowing how long she had spent entrenched in the darkness, but as she slowly regained her consciousness the crazy dream came flooding back to her, and she began to smile. At least she tried to smile, but quickly realised this was impossible, as her mouth and throat seemed to be filled with tubes.

"Well, that much is true anyways," she thought. "I have obviously had some kind of accident."

With difficulty she began to open her eyes. Yes, she was in a hospital bed, and apparently connected up to all manner of bleeping, whining and wheezing machinery. Within a few minutes the physical discomfort was beginning to turn to considerable pain, and it was with some relief that she saw a nurse come into the room.

"So, Mrs. Palmer, you've come back to us. That's good," and she seemed to adjust something out of sight and a blanket of warmth washed over Amanda pushing the pain into the distance. "That must be the morphine," she thought. And then a satisfied "ahhhhh."

"You had a nasty little turn. We thought we'd lost you. In fact we did lose you for a couple of minutes there, but Dr. Bennington brought you back. He's a lovely man you know, not like some of the other doctors. And handsome too . . . such a cute moustache . . ." She was now adjusting the sheets. Amanda tried to sit up, but her body didn't seem to be working.

"Now don't you try to move. You're not out of the woods yet you know." She was wandering around the room, checking on the various machines.

"Rest is what you need. Plenty of rest . . . And at your age these things can take a while." Now she was at the bottom of the bed, writing notes on a clipboard.

"Your family's been here the whole time. I think they've gone to get some breakfast. They'll be so pleased to see you're awake . . . And isn't Abigail a sweetheart . . . She's been my little helper these last few days."

Abigail? Did she know anyone called Abigail? She was becoming confused. Maybe it was the drugs. But then again, maybe she should expect a little confusion after what was obviously a serious accident of some kind or other.

The nurse seemed satisfied with the notes and clipped them back to the end of the bed. "I'm just going to tell Dr. Bennington you're awake," and she headed towards the door. Just before leaving she turned back to Amanda. "Yes, you have some very beautiful grandchildren. You must be very proud."

Did she hear that right? Grandchildren? She looked down across the bed. All she could see of her body was her hands. They looked old, frail, wrinkled and covered in veins . . . like the hands of an old lady . . . a 92 year old lady . . . And one word began to ring around her head, over and over . . .

"Fuck! fuck! fuck! fuck! fuck! fuck! FUCK! . . ."

A Personal Extroduction from Text Number Four

By ████████████████

Choosing a single example from the eight hundred and thirteen stories, poems and expositions I was given proved to be a very difficult process. After paring the collection down to 15 pieces I found myself having to invent various arbitrary criteria to aid my decision making. I discarded all those presented as poetry for no better reason than that I have always had issues with that form. Finally, having got it down to two, I was in something of a coin-toss scenario. I mention all this to emphasize that any small collection of this kind, gathered from so many rich and promising pieces will be by its very nature a somewhat unfair, arbitrary and random process, and should under no circumstances be considered authoritative. Personally I voted against the physical publication of this volume, preferring the compiling of an all-inclusive and thoroughly cross-referenced internet database, but I was outvoted, and not wishing to come across as a sore loser I decided to participate with all the thoroughness I could muster. (It was however agreed that I could express my many reservations about the project in this extroduction, as I have now done.)

I eventually settled on the previous story in large part because of its joie de vivre, an unusual and mildly ironic quality for a story focussing upon death, and to be honest, my best defence of this choice is simply that it tickled me somewhat. Strictly speaking the piece isn't really a *palmeresque* in the true sense of the word, but nonetheless the author was clearly very familiar with the *Amanda Palmer Circus*, that motley collection of cabaret artistes, dancers, musicians, midget acrobats, hangers on and devotedly organised (and fully costumerised) fans that travelled with her from gig to gig, town to town, in scenes reminiscent of nineteenth-century freak-shows. Indeed many on the editorial committee believe that the author was most likely an insider (either one of Amanda's friends or close colleagues) as there are a number of hidden references to small details of Amanda's personal life, such as quotes from her favourite books, not to mention the many more private references that could not have been known, nor recognised, by anyone outside the "inner sanctum". However none who have been asked have so far come forward, and it could well be that any story so rich in surreal symbolism will inevitably yield to retrospective interpretations of all kinds through nothing more than the subtle art of coincidence.

The writing is flamboyant, though strangely self-conscious, feeling the need to explain itself didactically from time to time. A number of the characters are clearly based, loosely and superficially, upon real people, indeed there is one that I suspect is a somewhat unflattering portrayal of myself. The author's portrayal of Amanda certainly depicts one aspect of her multifaceted personality fairly accurately, but is nonetheless rather flat and two dimensional, very much concerned with her constructed public face. There is nothing of the thoughtful, considered, sensitive, even vulnerable Amanda that those of us who knew her personally were familiar with. Nonetheless, the story is brimming over with vigour and optimism, and as such makes for a fitting memorial for an unquestionably colourful and energetic character. That is, in the first half. The second half seems to get stuck in an interminable, and rather tedious, debate with some form of super-ego figure posing as Nietzsche, but I let that pass on the strength of the first half alone.

I once asked Amanda how she would like to die. "In reality, or artistically?" she replied. "Artistically it would have to be something mysterious... maybe involving aliens or conspiracies... in reality, and this may seem a little disappointing, I'd probably like to die in bed, in my nineties, surrounded by family..." In this story she gets to try both.

If only real life could be that generous.

TEXT NUMBER FIVE

On the Unsung Death of Amanda Palmer

A poem for recitation in the manner of a vaudeville Melo-drama preferably with improvised dramatic piano accompaniment. The choruses should be sung by massed voices to the tune of "All Me Life I Wanted To Be Barrer Boy". The CHORUS should in general have their backs to the audience, turning to the front only to sing their lines, and then turning their backs once again.

CHORUS:
Who killed Amanda Palmer?
Who snatched her from our hearts?
Who stole away the best of us
To cleave the dream apart?

Who was it snuffed the candle?
Who damned us with that wrong?
Who plucked the flower before its bloom
Full ripened into song?

NARRATOR: *(Walking through the CHORUS to the front of the stage. He is reading to himself from a small black book of poetry. Then, suddenly he closes the book and addresses the audience.)*

And so it starts: the sun goes down
And city wide and city bright
The buzzing of fluorescent lights
Outweighs the dark and moonless sky
And all the silent passions drowned
By daylight's wilful sanity
And patience worn too thin, are free
To vent their pain about the town.

CHORUS:
They vent their pain about the town
They vent their pain about the town
Yes all the silent passions drowned
Now vent their pain about the town

NARRATOR: *(Raising his hands to the Heavens)*
Some say this is the end of days
Of History, of God, of Art
Of honour and restraint, all passed
Betrayed by that essential "now"
And "want" and "me" and "greed" and "lust":
Morality has lost its way
And we have drunk too much today.
                    (He looks down at the ground in despair)

CHORUS:
Oh we have drunk too much today
Yes we have drunk too much today
Morality has lost its way
For we have drunk too much today

NARRATOR: *(Raising his forefinger to the audience)*
Yet in that drunken overflow
That mad melee of lust and fight
That twists and scuffles, raining blows
Across the orange shadowed night

A gentle weeping found the heart
Of one whose sadness wandered by
And chanced upon a fearful sight:
(He staggers backwards, a look of shock in his eyes)
A little girl whose tears cried out
Amidst the city's dreadful shout
For sympathy and kindliness
And other friends whose time was passed.
(Once again he turns his eyes to the ground in despair)

CHORUS:
All other friends whose time has passed
Another friend whose time has passed
Yes sympathy and kindliness
Are all good friends whose time has passed

NARRATOR: *(Gesturing towards stage left)*
For there, beside her, at her feet
A crumpled mass of cloth and hair
And blood was pooling in the street
In silent gasps that found no air;
A person once, a woman, blest
With all the hopes of life to come,
Now chastened by the arms of Death
Cut short by hands whose dream was worth
But one more fix to help them numb
The pain of what they had become.
(He falls to his knees in an imitation of tragedy, his
                                        head in his hands)

CHORUS:
The pain of what they have become
The pain of what they have become
Just one more fix to help them numb
The pain of what they have become

NARRATOR: *(Still on his knees)*
And as she wept, that little girl
Her tears did mingle with the blood
And dirt and cans and cigarette stubs
That choke the gutters with despair
At all that had been done to her
And all that would be done again
For every evil known to Men
Is found within those stinking slums
Those dismal streets, those dreary paths
That mark our culture's epitaph.

CHORUS:
They mark our culture's epitaph
They mark our culture's epitaph
Those dismal streets and dreary paths
That mark our culture's epitaph

NARRATOR: *(He jumps suddenly to his feet, and ges-*
tures imploringly towards the audience)
He stood and watched, our passer-by
And though he felt, as well he might
A poet's soul within his heart
He watched the woman slowly die
Whilst twisting tight his fine moustache:
He acted not to soothe her pain
Nor comforted the weeping child
But stood in silence, helpless, drained
Of power by sudden fright, deprived
By cowardice of all he thought
He might have been, or could become:
He learnt His Truth, and that night wrought
His impotence in future songs.
> *(A look of dissolute cowardice on his face)*

CHORUS:
His impotence in future songs
His impotence in future songs
With a hey! and a ho! and a ding! Dang! Dong!
His impotence in future songs

NARRATOR: *(He gestures towards the chorus who*
have gathered in a crowd behind him, then turns to the front,
imploring once again)
He stood there as the sirens wailed
And soon a crowd had gathered round
The woman and the weeping child
But none would dare to step upon
The blood that spoke in eloquence
Of violence and its consequence.
No one reached forth to calm the girl
Whose freckled face and golden curls
Were smeared with blood and tears and bile
As in her arms she cradled all
That she could grasp of life now passed
A bundle made of arms and legs
And blood-soaked cloth.
    Till suddenly
A shout: Make way! Move back! Keep clear!
And men in uniforms were there
To sweep away the dreadful scene
Lest it offend the filth and sleaze,
Or mar the midnight reveries.

CHORUS:
Oh mar the midnight reveries
Let's mar the midnight reveries
Let's all offend the filth and sleaze
And mar the midnight reveries

NARRATOR: *(Searching, his hand shielding his eyes from the sun)*
But where, where went the weeping girl
With smearèd face and blood-soaked curls?
For none had seen her leave that place
Nor did the paramedics take
Her in their screaming ambulance
To file her name and stamp her heart
As "property of New York State"
It seemed as if she'd disappeared
And that was just a little weird.
(He paces back and forth across the stage, as if still searching)

CHORUS:
And that was just a little weird
Yes that was just a little weird
It seemed as if she'd disappeared
And that was just a little weird

NARRATOR: *(A change in tone, now more factual, addressing the audience)*
And so our poet passerby
Continued on his weary way
Much troubled by this weak response
When called upon; his impotence
To act when action was required.
What value poetry? he thought
When tragedy berates the heart
For letting such things come to pass.
What use to me is song and dance
If stand and stare is all I do
And think about the words I'll use
To make it mine, to take the scene
And frame it in bright poetry.
I am a coward and a rogue

Not worthy of the gifts bestowed
Upon me by the hands of Fate
I shall renounce my pen, and break
My staff upon the Heaven's gate.
> *(He raises his fist to the Heavens as if banging a great
> staff upon the Heaven's Gate)*

CHORUS:
He'll bang his staff upon the gate
His virile staff upon the gate
He shall renounce his pen, and break
His staff upon the Heaven's gate

NARRATOR: *(Looking down, as if taking a child's hand)*
But then a tiny voice, a hand
And looking down he saw the girl
But now her face was clean, her curls
Were bright, her dress no longer stained
"Mister," she said, "Do not be sad
Don't blame yourself for things you did
Or didn't do. There is no gain
In that. You didn't shoot the gun
You came upon her dead and gone."

CHORUS:
You came upon her dead and gone
You came upon her dead and gone
It wasn't you who shot the gun
You came upon her dead and gone

NARRATOR: *(Somewhat ashamed of himself)*
"But I . . . I acted not" said he
"I merely gazed upon the scene
To steal its essence as my own"
"Tush now" said she, and touched a bony
Finger to her sallow lips

"'Tis past. But I would ask you this
Please don't discard your poetry
But tell your tale and write of me
Of everything you saw this day
Of her who died in such a way . . ."

CHORUS:
Of her who died in such a way
Yes her who died in such a way
Tell everything you saw this day
Of her who died in such a way

NARRATOR: *(With kindness)*
"And what of you?" he asked. "What now
Where will you go, what will you do?
What is your name? Who cares for you?"
"Oh I was never really here
It was your poet's heart that found
A way to make my spirit's shape
My name is hers, her name is mine
In many ways we are the same
A single thought in different form:
I am her last unfinished song
A ghostly song conceived in death
And then abandoned, left unsung,
And so I ask of you kind sir
Please write me into tender verse
And spread my voice about the world
For that is still my destiny
If ever such a thing can be."

CHORUS:
If ever such a thing can be
If ever such a thing can be
Yes that is still my destiny
If ever such a thing can be

NARRATOR: *(Reassuring)*
"Oh, that's a promise I can keep
You have my word in certainty."
Then, in that instant, she was gone
She melted into melodies
That whispered ripples through the streets
Disguised upon the autumn breeze
A distant half remembered song

CHORUS:
A distant half remembered song
A distant half remembered song
Yes in that instant she was gone
A distant half remembered song

NARRATOR: *(He walks to the front of the stage. Once*
again a change in tone, now more factual, addressing the
audience.)
And so the poet wandered on
Not caring where his footsteps led
For he was lost in melodies
And words were dancing round his head
Until he landed home at last
And set about the promised task.
    (He takes a pen and paper from his pocket and starts
to write)

CHORUS:
He set about the promised task
He set about the promised task
Oh when he landed home at last
He set about the promised task

NARRATOR: *(As if telling a story)*
For five long days he sat and wrote
And wrote and sat and did not care

For sustenance, nor did he fear
The fever rising in his bones
'Till, as he penned the final word
His heart gave out, a groan was heard
Then nothing and the poet died
His promise kept, his oath preserved.

CHORUS:
His promise kept, his oath preserved
His promise kept, his oath preserved
He'd written out his final word
His promise kept, his oath preserved

NARRATOR:
For five long weeks his body lay
Unnoticed by the world around
Until his landlord came to claim
The money that the poet owed
And opening the door he found
A stinking corpse upon the ground.
But even selling everything
The poet owned, his books, his ring
His shabby clothes, his summer tent
There's not enough to pay the rent.

CHORUS:
There's not enough to pay the rent
No not enough to pay the rent
His shabby clothes, his summer tent
Were not enough to pay the rent

NARRATOR: *(Very moral tone)*
And so they cleared away the mess
And found upon the dead man's desk
A manuscript, an epic verse

That told of tragedies and woes:
How Poverty was raped by vice
Left bleeding in the street to die
And yet, a seed was sown, a life
Was made, a story born of song
To heal the heart that broke so long
Ago; to salve the festering wound
That marks our hearts within the womb.

CHORUS:
They mark our hearts within the womb
They mark our hearts within the womb
Those self-inflicted festering wounds
That mark our hearts within the womb

NARRATOR:
And as they cleared away the mess
They took the papers from his desk
And bagged them up with rotten food
And other rubbish from the room
And no one ever read the lines
That broke his heart, for which he died,
For in a dumpster they were put
And in a landfill now they rot.

CHORUS:
And in a landfill now they rot
And in a landfill now they rot
For in a dumpster they were put
And in a landfill now they rot

NARRATOR:
And soon a pretty girl moved in
Who had a job, and paid the rent
On time, and no one spoke of him

Again, who died where now she brings
Her clients for nightly spanking fun
And other corporate disciplines.
(Finally he turns his head away in despair, and walks,
through the CHORUS off stage right.)

CHORUS:
Who killed Amanda Palmer?
Who snatched her from our hearts?
Who stole away the best of us
To cleave the dream apart?

Who was it snuffed the candle?
Who damned us with that wrong?
Who plucked the flower before its bloom
Full ripened into song?
Who plucked the flower before its bloom
Full ripened into song?

A Personal Extroduction from Text Number Nine

By ███████████

Initially I was quick to discard this piece as it is in many ways not really a *palmeresque* at all, however it caused me such ironic amusement that in the end I found myself returning to it repeatedly for light relief during the arduous reading process. Finally, and quite unexpectedly, I found it had become my choice.

I am still uncertain quite how seriously it is intended: I like to think that the author was entirely unaware of the comic potential of his/her work (the work itself implies that the author is male), although I suspect it was knowingly calculated, largely due to the faintly mocking tone of the chorus sections. It is very much a piece that only really works when read aloud, as the high register of the language seems clunky and exaggerated on the page but proves great fun to perform. I imagine it being read aloud at some Victorian fireside, vastly overacted, and the whole family joining in the chorus sections.

The narrative of the piece is interesting in a number of ways, some of them most likely unintentional or possibly again cleverly contrived. Essentially it seems to be a glorification of the poet himself. The poet stumbles accidentally upon the dying Miss Palmer and there finds himself paralysed by the sight, unable to help or assist in any real way. But then the spirit of Miss Palmer's creativity is passed from her dying body to him, and he vows to make something in verse worthy of the terrible sight he has encountered, to make art from her death. He returns home and writes a masterpiece, but alas it is never read as he dies upon concluding, the power of his own words having literally broken his heart, and since he owes money for his rent his possessions are hastily cleared and discarded for the next tenant. Thus it seems to ask the questions: is Art of any real value compared to the realities of Life and Death?; is a great poem still a great poem if it is never read?; can inaction when action is necessary ever be redeemed through Artistic creation? But there is also a proto-literary twist, for it is hinted at that the poem we are reading is the poet's great work, but that was supposed to have been lost, and if it is then who finished it? Who wrote of the poet's death? Or is it essentially a poem about the making of the great poem? A making-of docu-verse?

But in the end the narrative itself had little to do with why I chose this particular piece – I chose it because of that charmingly ludicrous image I had of a stern Victorian father reciting aloud at the fireside, his children chiming in with every chorus. Television has indeed got a lot to answer for.

TEXT NUMBER SIX

On the Aesthetic Decline of the Mock-Funeral

One of the stranger fashions to have been taken up by the wealthy and celebrated in recent years is that of staging one's own funeral. And indeed it is a great illustration of how we, the readers of tabloid newspapers and glossy magazines, can become acclimatised to that which is absurd, bizarre and utterly extraordinary. The other day, whilst standing in a supermarket queue, I overheard a conversation between two middle-aged and somewhat overweight women flicking through *Zoo* magazine. Suddenly the elder of the two said, "Ooh, they've got Ozzie's funeral". The other leant over to take a look. "How many goats did he have?" After a brief pause the first replied "Sixteen, and four ostriches. . . . Eddie Izzard was the priest." They turned the page. "Oh, doesn't Kelly look gorgeous in black." "I bet those shoes cost a fortune." Then one pointed at some picture I couldn't see and they both erupted in laughter. "Did she really think she could get away with that! . . ." "J-Lo's was better, more colourful." I was fascinated by the casualness with which they discussed what I felt to be a considerably surreal event. To them it was little more than a fashion parade, an excuse to admire and condemn the tastes and figures of younger, richer, prettier people than themselves; to me it was an expression of unprecedented decadence amongst the celebrity classes, and, as with all expressions of decadence, a most revealing window to the many hidden (and not so hidden) sicknesses within.

This unlikely fashion for the premature staging of one's own death ritual should not be confused with the ancient rituals of rebirth that are known to date back to the days of the Pharaohs, if not earlier. Those were part of a larger whole, a manifestation of religious beliefs that placed the political leader in the role of a God, whose rebirth on a monthly, or in some cases daily, cycle was deemed to be essential for the health of society. Their political purpose was the demonstration of hierarchy, and the reinforcement of power bases. They remained fixed and unchanged across generations. By contrast, this modern manifestation is an expression of individual concerns and values and though it naturally relates to issues within the larger society it is essentially a personalised ritual, in most cases designed as a public display of the aesthetic or philosophy of what I shall refer to as the "notionally deceased".

To fully grasp the essence of the mock-funeral it is important to contemplate for a moment the essence of a real funeral, that being, at least in today's society, the cathartic expression of grief. A funeral without grief is essentially an empty vessel, devoid of meaning or motivation, and it is that vacuum which lies at the heart of the mock-funeral. How it is filled, be it with statements of aesthetic, commercial implications, protest, egotism or simply fashion, can be a very telling indicator of the spiritual and indeed mental health and concerns not just of the persons involved, but also of the times in which they live.

Let us consider for how this all started. The earliest known example of a mock-funeral being staged purely for aesthetic or artistic reasons is that of Frances Featherstone in 1894. Featherstone, a self proclaimed *pre-modernist*[1] poet of the late nineteenth century and spiritual leader of the movement known as the *Devon-*

---

[1]   Featherstone is first known to have used this term in a letter to his friend, Emily Watson, dated January 21st 1891. The original letter now resides in the collection of St. Ambrose College, Exeter.

shire Cathartists, became, towards the end of his life, increasingly fixated upon the crucifixion and subsequent resurrection of Jesus, despite being an ardent atheist and proudly devout sinner. On July 4th 1894, before a crowd of around thirty fellow poets and other pre-modernist artists, he was ritually enshrouded and be-coffined, placed upon a pauper's hearse and pulled, by his followers, eight miles into the depths of Dartmoor, to a ready dug grave. The coffin was interred at midday, fires were lit, toasts were given and Featherstone's epic poem, *Reinventing Lazarus* (now sadly lost) was recited by Sir Henry Irving, with occasional breaks for light refreshments. Finally, upon completion of the recitation some twelve or so hours later, the grave was unfilled and Featherstone arose from the ground at midnight, cleansed and renewed, miraculously reborn through Art. At least that is how the event is presented in his journal.[2] A local newspaper[3] report paints a slightly different picture:

This last Sunday was witnessed a further demonstration of the increasing lunatic eccentricity of local "character" Frances Featherston[sic.] and his dubious associates. In what can only be described as a most perplexing comedy of sanctimony Featherstone had himself be-coffined amid considerable invented ceremony, and then dragged upon an offall[sic.] cart into the depths of the moor. Our source, who followed the proceedings at what was described as a respectable distance, reports that upon arrival atop Crow Tor the coffin was placed in a ready dug grave and covered over, following which the most debaucherous of celebrations ensued involving much drunkenness and not inconsiderable nudity. Among the revellers were the actor Henry Irving and Exeter stationary magnate Sir Edmond Whitstable . . . What possible motive he might have had for such an act of assured self-importance is hard to

---

[2]   Featherstone's journal number 16, page 161.
[3]   The *Totness Times*, February 29th, 1894.

fathom, but one would have thought Mr. Featherston[sic.]
would be keeping a low profile given the recent allegations
levelled against him . . .

Whichever account is closer to the actual occasion, it is clear
that the proceedings were conducted with considerable ritual intention, and it should be noted that even drunken nudity would
not be undertaken lightly in February on Dartmoor where tem-
peratures frequently fall well below freezing. Featherstone's journal[4] indicates that his intention was that of rebirth:

. . . and through this act I shall arise reborn, cleansed of all
that has corroded my soul over a life unduly devoted t'wards
sin, corruption and vice . . .

However overblown, romanticised and egotistical this may
seem, it must be acknowledged that ritual rebirth is at least a fitting purpose to motivate a mock-funeral, and is in many ways expressive of the aesthetic of the *fin de siecle* as a whole. This was
after all a period whose artistic movements were dominated by
Mme. Blavatsky's pseudo-spiritualism, consumption of opium and
absinthe, and a faith in social progress not yet undermined by the
savage mechanisation of war. Featherstone was attempting to free
himself of his past persona, to make himself a better man, and
ultimately to prepare himself for his final act of contrition—the
self-crucifixion of 1896 that was to inspire a generation of future
artists.

Featherstone himself had certainly never intended to start a
trend. As a man dedicated to uniquenesses of expression, he would
most likely have been scornful toward those he often described as
"nature's harmless copyists". However, among the then-fashion-
able *Decadent* movement of artists, this ritual of rebirth through
artistic debauchery was widely taken up. In the following years

---

4   Journal number 16, page 156.

there are many such accounts of mock-funerals, each of them following something of the same pattern. Count Eric Von Stenbock, Franz Stuck, Ernest Dowson, M.P. Shiel, and Octave Mirbeau are all known to have conducted mock-funerals that largely followed the same pattern as Featherstone's, specifically including recitations, drunkenness and nudity; though in none of the above cases did the notionally-deceased spend more than an hour nailed within the coffin.

Among the more notable figures to plan such an event at that time was Featherstone's one time friend, and long time enemy (following a much publicised argument involving accusations of plagiarism on Featherstone's part) Oscar Wilde. Until recently it was assumed that Wilde had planned this event to mark a ritual rebirth after his all too public disgrace, however recently discovered letters[5] strongly imply that it was in fact planned more as a satire on Featherstone's own self-importance. Either way it was widely anticipated as a most elaborate event, due to take place on January 1st, 1901. Sadly Wilde's actual death on November 30th 1900 cut these plans short, and the lack of funds left upon his decease resulted in a plain and non-descript real funeral most memorable for the moment when "Bosey" Douglas, Wilde's lover and instrument of his downfall, was accidentally knocked into the open grave by Father Cuthbert Dunne.

The unprecedented death toll of World War One brought an abrupt end to this first wave of mock-funerals, particularly after the unfortunately timed event staged by the minor English painter Edgar Stanhope in November 1916 which resulted in a mob chasing the participants along Brighton's London Road, whilst hurling both abuse and horse dung.[6] At a time when many families were deprived of the closure of a real funeral for their lost brothers,

---

[5]   These letters were found in a small box stowed in the attic of his family home at 21 Westland Row, Dublin, in 1996, and remain in the possession of his family.

[6]   *Brighton Evening Argus*, November 17th, 1916, page 4.

fathers and lovers such self-indulgent stagings were deemed to be in considerable bad taste, a mood that continued between the wars and on into the years of depression and austerity. This consensus was however broken by two notable exceptions, those being Ezra Pound and Aleister Crowley, both men who took great delight in affronting polite society and challenging what they considered, each in their own way, to be the "woolly thinking of the bourgeoisie".

In the case of Ezra Pound this was an opportunistic event. Shortly after his arrival in Paris in April 1920 he was walking with his friend, Dadaist artist Marcel Duchamp, through the grand cemetery of Père Lachaise when they noticed that the grave of Oscar Wilde had been partially dug open to lay the foundations for the monument by Jacob Epstein that had been commissioned by Wilde's friend Robert Ross. Such an opportunity could not be missed and so they returned later that evening with a veritable coterie of Parisian artists and writers to perform what can only be described as a modernist satire of the pre-war mock-funeral. Gertrude Stein described the scene in a letter to her brother[7]:

> . . . having been wrapped in a pink flowered bedspread, and very much playing the part of a cadaver, Ezra was placed in an old pine wardrobe, for a coffin had been impossible to acquire at short notice, and was carried from the gates to Wilde's grave, where the box was placed in the shallow hole at something of an angle, for it did not quite fit. There Marcel took the role of the priest with great gusto, declaring hellfire and damnation upon the assembled crowd before turning toward the grave itself and reciting an improvised and somewhat comical eulogy to the Romantic arts concluding with

---

[7]   This letter, now lost, was published in an article entitled "The influence of the death of Oscar Wilde upon the evolution of the Dadaist movement" by the eminent art historian Dietricht Hossbaum, *Archipelago* magazine, Spring 1961.

the words: "and so we lay to rest all that was decadent and corrupted, overblown and weighted down with unnecessary emotion that now might rise the pure essence of Art, unencumbered by the drivel and bile that held it down for so very long . . ." or words to that effect. At this the wardrobe door creaked open and up popped Ezra, grinning inanely, only to disappear inside the wardrobe and reappear repeatedly, each time wearing a differently coloured wig or false beard, and on each occasion drawing great cheers from the assembled crowd. Then suddenly the cemetery authorities arrived and there ensued a most comical chase amongst the tombs with the wardrobe being carried aloft, and Ezra, still sat within, heaping grandiloquent curses upon the guards for having the udacity to disturb such a sacred event . . .[8]

By contrast Crowley's mock-funeral, conducted on December 1st, 1937, appropriately ten years to the day before his actual death, was by all accounts a most serious and earnest event, however it is impossible to know exactly what took place as each of the six surviving accounts differ considerably, and unravelling the many possibilities would demand a book in itself. Certainly it was a vividly occult affair, with ritual robes and recitations; and one thing we can be fairly sure of is that some form of animal sacrifice was involved, although whether it was three chickens, a goat or a marmoset depends upon which account, if any, you choose to believe.

All of the above examples, whether satirical or in earnest, share a concern with aesthetic and artistic ideologies in the place of grief. The 1960s saw the rise of a new kind of mock-funeral; one that focussed instead upon political ideologies, in which the notionally deceased was a non-participant, or even, by the later 1960s, an idea. The first known example of this new form of funerary expression came about during the nomination process of

---

[8]   Translated from the original French.

the 1960 US presidential campaign. John F. Kennedy was initially challenged for the democratic nomination by Hubert Humphrey, who was to later become Vice President under Lyndon B. Johnson. As if to emphasize the age of his opponent, followers of the (relatively) young Senator Kennedy began regularly staging the mock-funeral of Senator Humphrey, culminating in a mass mock-funeral in West Virginia with over ten thousand participants and, unusually, over twenty coffins, each emblazoned with Humphrey RIP in vivid red paint upon the side. Some commentators consider this to have been a major contribution towards Kennedy's victory. Following the success of this campaign the mock-funeral became a staple of the various protest movements that characterised the latter half of the sixties, with the notionally deceased representing variously democracy, freedom, black rights, capitalism, and animal welfare among other ideologies. However, as the various political assassinations of that decade began to pile up the mock-funeral took on a sense of threat that soon attracted the attention of government legislators. This situation came to a head when right wing white activists staged a mock-funeral for Martin Luther King Jr. on January 8th, 1968, one week before his actual assassination. As a result mass political mock-funerals were banned in the US in a bill passed later that year.[9] This led to a somewhat surreal campaign in which mock-funerals were held where the notionally deceased was the mock-funeral itself.

Certainly this political use of the mock-funeral is an interesting chapter in its history, however, in the opinion of the author

---

[9]   This bill was finally overturned in January 2007 in time for the National Association for the Advancement of Coloured People to hold a much publicised mock-funeral for the word "nigger", the only known example of such an event being held for a word, and, ironically, an event which led to a considerable upsurge in the use of the "N" word in reports of that same event, and thereafter, as the reports themselves seemed to have somehow legitimised the use of the word by people who had hitherto deemed it politically incorrect and indeed offensive.

they deviate so far from the true essence of the form that they should be more properly referred to as quasi-mock-funerals. These are expressions of mass political movements and a symptom of a mass society that sacrifices individuality upon the alter of political intent, thereby actively turning its back upon the true nature of the tradition as established by Featherstone. The true mock-funeral, like its real counterpart should be an expression of individuality, even more so than the real funeral as there is no need to contain grief within comforting bland formalities.

The second great wave of aesthetically motivated mock-funerals dates back to the early 1970s. Interestingly the first wave had been developed and performed largely among poets whereas this second wave seems to have been taken up almost exclusively amongst popular musicians. It has been suggested by some that this handover represents further evidence of the increasing bastardisation of contemporary artistic culture, however, others (misguidedly in the opinion of the author) claim that "pop stars" are today's poets and therefore the link is self evident.

This second wave began in April 1971 with Jim Morrison. Morrison had moved to Paris in March of that year and was in the habit of taking long walks through Père Lachaise cemetery. Very much a literarily minded character he had read of Pound's performance at Wilde's grave and is known to have always kept an eye out for a similarly unfilled grave on his strollings. On April 2nd he found just such a hole and immediately gathered up a number of friends, and indeed a wardrobe, this time made of mahogany, to restage the event. According to Wally Eiselworth[10] (a close friend of Pamela Courson, Morrison's long term lover) who was present at the event, everything went to plan until Morrison attempted to climb into the wardrobe. It seems that he was suffering from a distinct excess of alcohol at the time, and, having put on a considerable amount of weight in the previous six months, he became

---

[10]   From an interview in the television programme "The Death of Jim Morrison", ABC Television, 1997.

stuck in the wardrobe door at which point a cemetery guard arrived. His friends attempted to lift the wardrobe with the intention of making a quick getaway but the immense weight of the mahogany plus Morrison's own not inconsiderable girth meant that they only managed around five yards before the wardrobe was dropped, unfortunately trapping the flared trouser leg of Alain Ronay. The others ran and hid amongst the cemetery furniture and thus it was in this unfortunate position, (Morrison trapped in a broken wardrobe and Ronay urgently attempting to remove his pinioned trousers), that Morrison and Ronay were arrested, although ultimately no charges were pressed.

This abortive attempt at conducting a mock-funeral may seem to have made no contribution to the tradition itself, and indeed it would not have done had Jonah Roe not been among the notional mourners. Although not a musician himself, Roe was part of "the scene" and by all accounts was a charming young man who was "adopted" by a series of notable pop stars and other artists throughout the seventies and eighties due in large part to his exceptional ability to memorise almost everything he read. According to Ian Hunter, lead singer of the band Mott the Hoople, he was "a veritable font of the quirky and bizarre"[11] and became a much sought after companion and dinner guest amongst the great, the good and the eminently artistically fashionable. Distantly descended from a family of Neapolitan princes he was easily recognised by the fine waxed false moustache he always wore, apparently due to the fact that every second generation of his family was unable to grow a real moustache (he was of that second generation, and this was his rebellion). It was Roe who initially introduced Morrison to the story of Pound's mock-funeral, and a decade later he would do the same for David Bowie, adding, much to the amusement of his dining companions, a vigorously demonstrated portrayal of Morrison's re-enactment. It seems likely that it was this evening's story-telling that inspired Bowie's own mock-funeral in January 1983.

----

[11]   Ibid.

A true mock-funeral in every sense, Bowie's intention was to bury his previous more psychedelic, experimental and drug-fuelled stage and recording personae, and to thus draw a line under his years contracted to RCA. Conducted in the grounds of his Swiss home, the Château de Mésanges in Upper Lausanne, the ritual was performed before an invited audience which included many figures of note from the artier end of the popular music scene, such as Iggy Pop, Brian Eno, Elton John, Roger Daltry, and Lou Reed, among others. Since the funeral was not for Bowie himself, but for a number of invented personae, the coffin was filled with various stage costumes, demo tapes and an electric guitar which had been used on the "Ziggy Stardust" tour. Bowie himself played the role of priest, dressed in a costume extravagantly based upon Tintoretto's painting of Pope Alexander IV. Not wishing to be out-done Elton John dressed as the Angel of Death (by all accounts more flamboyant angel than death) and Iggy Pop dressed as Jesus on the cross, although he abandoned the cross itself halfway through the procession. Always a canny businessman Bowie had invited photographer Justin de Villeneuve (real name Nigel Davies) to photograph the event and the pictures were sold for a substantial sum to *Pose!* magazine. The Château was sold in 1992 and in recent years the current owners have dug up considerable portions of the grounds in the hope of finding the coffin and its contents, so far with no success.

On June 12th, 1994 Elton John was to take up the baton in what was, at the time, the most publicised (and indeed the most extravagant) mock-funeral ever to have been conducted. The ritual itself was intended to celebrate John's "coming out" as an openly gay man, and to finally bury his many years of pretence and inhibition. It was therefore, by necessity, an extraordinarily camp affair culminating in the now iconic moment when six white swans took to the air lifting the lid of the casket and John arose from within, reborn, wearing nothing but a gold plated loin cloth, which some journalists unfairly described as a "gilded nappy". Many commentators credit this event with inspiring the current fashion for mock-funerals, and given the wide media coverage and host of celebrities present this does seem to be a likely analysis. Among those attending were numerous film stars, pop stars, fashion designers, super-models, and a vast array of funerary professionals performing the roles of undertakers and mutes (official mourners) to lead the not so sombre procession. The proceedings were filmed by MTV and the photographs appeared in numerous gossip and glamour magazines. The video footage remains to this day among the top 100 most watched clips on the website YouTube.

Following this most theatrical of events it seems the mould was set and, despite the essential ritual meaning behind Mr. John's "memorial to past unnecessary restraints" it was sadly (though in retrospect perhaps inevitably, given society's current obsessions) the fashion and celebrity spectacle elements that took root. What started with a slow and steady drip during the late 1990s, with mock-funerals being conducted for public display every six months or so by "B-list" celebrities keen for magazine exposure (Gaby Roslin, Cilla Black, Richard Madeley, Jonathan Ross, Jordan, and Paris Hilton among others), has now grown to a steady stream. Rarely does a week pass without some gossip-rag or other boasting exclusive picture rights, and all notions of meaning and purpose have been discarded in favour of celebrity glamour. Even the ritual itself has been largely sidelined with the host's be-coffined arrival upon a horse-drawn hearse often being the only nod to what was once a powerful statement of transition and rebirth.

Of course, no discussion of mock-funerals would be complete without mentioning the tragic case of Amanda Palmer. As a songstress who rose to the celebrity "C-lists" during the early 2000s she attended a number of such events and by all accounts was increasingly disturbed by what she viewed as the dumbing down of a great and venerable institution. In a letter to the *New York Times* in March 2002 she wrote:

. . . It seems that today even the most private and personal of moments are being reduced to their potential for publicity amongst the exhibitionist classes and the ravenous public that feeds upon them... I, alas, like so many in my profession, am guilty on both sides...[12]

The following June she decided to stage a mock-funeral herself as a protest against her own participation in what she referred to as "the ever-growing Amanda Palmer circus".[13] In a phone call that morning to a friend, who has asked to remain anonymous, she explained that she would be doing it alone, with no media, no fans, no costumes, not even any friends present as the very notion of an audience would betray her intentions. It was to be a private ritual, to cleanse herself of the taint of hypocrisy and superficiality that she had recently been railing against at every much publicised opportunity. She made no mention of the location for fear of word getting out to the very people she was ritually attempting to free herself from. Four days later her body was found in a field near Bellmans Creek off the New Jersey Turnpike. It seems that she had propped the coffin against the side of partially dug makeshift grave and then climbed inside. At some point the coffin had toppled over, lid downwards, leaving her unable to escape and she had suffocated. The coroner recorded a verdict of death by misadventure, stating specifically that there was no evidence that suggested any indication of foul play or intention of suicide. At the head of the grave was a wooden board with the words "Here lies the vanity of youth compounded by the hypocrisy of age" burnt into it with a soldering iron.

This remains to this day the only known example of a fatality caused directly through the enacting of a mock-funeral.

---

12   *New York Times*, March 22nd 2002.
13   Ibid.

A Personal Extroduction from Text Number Six

By ████████████

Well this certainly isn't a true *palmeresque*, or really any kind of *palmeresque*, but having read over eight hundred of the damn things, most of them very similar, derivative and frankly pretty poor, this positively leapt from the page at me, screaming "at last, something different, with a bit of imagination!" I was immediately taken with the format: that of an academic essay complete with footnotes and yet describing something obviously invented and largely absurd—not an approach I have come across before, and delivered with considerable confidence and some occasional flair.

Overall it is a highly original, and at best, wonderfully comic piece, although at times the academic tone is in danger of becoming a touch arch. As a literary venture it is ambitious, setting itself up, as it does, as a pastiche of celebrity that functions both as *homage* and critique of the genre, but largely succeeds in juggling these two functions without dropping either ball. The piece is often wildly inventive and very amusing, the formality of its tone and the *faux* references only adding to its sense of veracity—the reader is never quite fooled but occasionally he/she does start to think "Well, yes, this *could* have happened" (the use of real names is partly responsible for this, and the author's evident knowledge of the different cultural movements that have dominated the last hundred years also helps create authenticity).

The piece explores, indeed is obsessed with, ideas of authorship, invention and imitation; the purity of artistic invention and its subsequent debasement through ever more ignorant derivations. The writing style itself is very confident and draws together influences from the Romantic tradition, the Gothic, HP Lovecraft, Poe, Blake, Baudelaire, the macabre, and the supernatural. Despite the essay format, the tease at the top combined with the historic chronological pattern creates an overall strong narrative drive.

But most of all it is the subject itself that attracted me: the notion of the ritualised staging of one's own mock funeral replete with artistic intentions, bells and smells. I am certainly tempted. And it would be the perfect opportunity for me to wear that papal robe I had made last year. Hmmm . . .

On the Unreported Death of Amanda Palmer

Like so many other twelve-year-old girls Amanda Palmer dreamt of fame, celebrity and fashionable parties. However, unlike so many other twelve-year-old girls, by the age of seventeen she had it all; and unlike so many others who had it all, it really did seem to be everything she had ever dreamt of. But seeming isn't being, and youth is a dangerous thing for it knows no endings. To the young Amanda this was just the beginning; to the cruel hand of Fate her ride was soon to be over. Had she been older and wiser she would have noticed the signs, she would have been watching for them. As it was she bathed each day in the adoration of her fans and read her soul in celebrity magazines. The world had become her magic mirror, and she truly was the fairest of them all.

Certainly she had worked hard to get there; nobody could deny that. From the age of five she had been dancing and singing at various after-school and Saturday clubs and had spent every spare minute practising the skills that had ultimately catapulted her to semi-stardom. And she had missed out on so much along the way. In place of friends she had had rivals; in place of play she had had hard work; in place of love she had had stern encouragement; and in place of education she had had ceaseless scales and dance-steps. But in the end it had all been worth it. She had steered her steady course toward glamour and celebrity and now, finally, she had arrived. And how she did love the glamour of it all: the exclusive invitations, the famous faces, the flash of cameras and the screaming fans; why, even buying a pint of milk from the corner store had become a thrilling adventure. Just so did her youth slowly pass upon a merry-go-round of concerts, parties, hotels, paparazzi and the steady adoration of her devoted audience. But alas, had she looked up glamour in a dictionary she would have known it was nothing but a hollow enchantment, a spell cast upon the naive and unwary by those potent forces who silently plot in the background, maintaining the status quo whilst making themselves oh-so-very rich.

Meanwhile, each morning at 10am her assistant, Jamie, arrived wherever she happened to be staying, with coffee and the morning's press cuttings and magazines. These she read through with all the enthusiasm of a child on Christmas morning, and with every photograph, every mention of her name, her colour seemed to ripen, just a touch. But then one day, on a crisp October morning in Seattle, at the age of 27, the previously unthinkable happened.

"Jamie . . ." There was the smallest hint of anxiety in her voice. "Jamie!"

An over-enthusiastic and richly moustachioed young man entered the sitting room of her hotel suite through a Japanese-style sliding screen, although on this occasion his enthusiasm was channelled more towards cowering.

"Jamie. Have you got this morning's cuttings?"

"Erm . . . no Amanda . . . We couldn't get hold of . . . errr . . . there's been a problem . . . with the delivery . . ."

Amanda gave him a look, the kind of look that is impossible to describe but were you ever to receive such a look you would know it immediately.

"Are you lying to me, Jamie?"

He seemed to stoop just a little lower, and cast his eyes to the floor.

"Err . . . yes Amanda."

"Well what the . . . ! Is there something you don't want me to see?"

"Yes . . . and no . . ."

"Then spit it out boy!"

"There weren't any." The words burst out like the cap on an over-pressurised boiler.

"What?"

"There weren't any."

"What? . . . not any?"

"Not a single one."

"What? . . . but that's . . . impossible! . . . not even . . ."

"Not even the smallest, most cursory of sideways back-handed comments. Not one." Now he was beginning to enjoy the moment, though not so you, or rather she, would have noticed.

"Oh," and her face seemed to measurably contort as if trying to fit around the alien idea. In the silence that followed it was easy to imagine the creaking sound a wooden bridge might make in the moments before its collapse. Then suddenly the room erupted in a chaos of shouts and breakages. Jamie had seen this happen many times before and wasn't the least bit thrown. Experience had taught him to stand back, wait for the inevitable exhausted calm and then address the situation. He glanced at his watch. Later he would note how long the tantrum had lasted in his diary.

Now she was in tears. Six minutes, forty two seconds. The calm would be here soon.

When it arrived, ten minutes, thirty seven seconds after her tantrum had started, she was sat on the edge of the sofa, rocking back and forth repeating over and over "What am I going to do?... What am I going to do?" Jamie looked down at her. She was visibly paler, and seemed somehow smaller than before. He sat next to her on the sofa, reaching across with a comforting arm, and at its touch she crumpled into him. He cherished these brief moments, and took a minute to soak it up.

"Right," said Jamie, suddenly appearing decisive and authoritative. "The first thing we do is get you a new publicist. Hell, let's get you a whole firm of publicists. That'll be all it needs. You know how the game works. We'll simply up the ante." And then he launched into a stream of uplifting rhetoric which, though utterly meaningless and therefore not worthy of presentation here, she nonetheless found most comforting and he considerably enjoyed purporting.

The following afternoon at 2:15pm they were sitting on expensive chairs in a large and rather plush office of the PR firm of Alcott & Filch. Mr. Filch himself was holding forth before them, explaining laboriously the many benefits of hiring his company. After five minutes Amanda impatiently butted in.

"So okay, we've had the hard sell, you're on . . . so what's the plan? What can you do? . . ."

"Hmmmm." Mr Filch leant back in his chair and stretched out his legs. He smiled, just a little, causing his weaselly grey moustache to turn up awkwardly at the ends, and the large boil on his nose to redden. "Well, Miss Palmer, we can certainly get you back at the centre of things, for a time, but you have to understand, as with everything else, there are natural laws that govern the publicity industries. These can be bent, pushed to the very limits, but ultimately they cannot be broken. I am a great publicist, possibly even the best, but I am not a god. I can manipulate, but I cannot control . . ." Here he paused, for dramatic reasons.

"As I see it, your assets are worn out. Sure, you still have your talent, and your looks, for now, but nobody cares anymore. Been there, done that, got the t-shirt, the CDs, the biographies and memoirs and photo-albums, the dress-up dollies . . . However extraordinary you may once have been, you have now been normalised. The quirkiness that once excited so much interest has become a tired cliché . . . It's time to change the brand! Be dangerous again, unpredictable . . . go crazy, murder your mother, no, scrap that one . . . but do something utterly unexpected and out of character. I can get the cameras there. What happens next is up to you. But make it good. If you're gonna maintain their interest it'll have to be good. And you must be prepared to follow through . . . Think about it and get back to me." And with that he turned to the side, picked up the phone and dialled a number. "And make it soon. Every day you're out of the scene makes it trickier. I'll be hearing from you." Then he turned his back entirely and began talking on the phone, making it clear that the meeting was over.

For the following week Amanda kept herself largely unobtainable only deigning to see Jamie briefly each morning for any updates, but alas, no press cuttings. It was as if the tap had suddenly been turned off; not even the smallest of drips leaking out to pool at the grungy bottom of the sink. Whilst Jamie got on with the job of running the company that *was* Amanda Palmer, its namesake sat and sulked and mused and brooded as only a gifted prima-donna ever could. But even she eventually tired of self-pity, and by day ten of anonymity her resolve was complete: she would have to become dangerous, unpredictable . . . She would sell her soul to Alasdair Filch. It was her only real option, or so she felt.

The next day they were back on the expensive chairs in Filch's office. Amanda leant forward to sign the theatrically oversized contract on Filch's desk. Filch himself was sat bolt upright, gently tapping the tips of his fingers together, barely able to disguise the look of glee in his eyes, though his mouth remained reassuringly sour. Jamie sat back in his chair, a slightly concerned look upon his face, as if he had the smallest of reservations about the proceedings.

"So," declared Filch, "Welcome to the family." And he snatched up the contract, briefly checked the signatures and then placed it in a draw. "Well, let's get started then. I suggest we set about this with some degree of urgency. Let's say Friday. Get yourself down to *Butter* in New York, you know, the club. Hilton and Lohan will be there, and doubtless numerous other pap-hunters, has-beens and wannabes. Check out who's around, choose the most popular girl you can find and create a few minor scenes with her during the night. Keep it down though, you wanna just set the pan on the hob, don't let it boil over. Then, as you're leaving, turn it into a cat-fight. Try to get the other girl to throw the first punch if you can, but if not no matter. I'll see to it that the cameras are there; spread a few rumours or something . . . You just make it good, and believable . . . And make sure they get the pictures they want. Get your skirt ripped off or something if you can. But not boobs. We're not ready for that yet . . . yes, keep them in reserve for now . . . But some kind of wardrobe malfunction could be good . . . I guarantee you double page spreads if you get it right. Excellent! Let's meet again then on Monday at 11 to discuss the results." And the meeting was over.

And so on Friday night Amanda found herself stalking cele-brettes at *Butter*. She had easily overcome her initial reservations about the plan, and indeed Jamie's, after all he was really just a minion; his opinion was only occasionally required, and even less frequently acknowledged. He was under strict instructions to wait by the exit and not to interfere under any circumstances. She was treating the evening as a piece of improvised theatre, and as such had entirely emotionally disconnected from the events she was about to instigate. Of course, being Amanda Palmer, Manda as the press liked to call her, she could approach anyone she liked without fear of cold shoulders. But who should she play? Who would make the best victim to her manipulations? Who was the most popular amongst this evening's many celebrettes? . . . And then she saw her principle target. Madonna, Princess Madge her-self. Perfect. So much to provoke her with. Her age alone would probably be enough. And it might mean she leaves earlier than some of the more youthful amongst her fellows. Yes, that would indeed be perfect, and she made her way towards the crowd of wannabes, wannabeseenwiths and other glamour-moths that sur-rounded Madonna. She elbowed her way through.

"Madge my dear, so good to see you, you look awesome!"

"Oh, Amanda, what fun." And they did the whole French mock double kiss thing.

"No really, you look fantastic. I mean, look at the two of us. Who'd ever guess you were twice my age?" And so the baiting began. Over the following few hours Amanda truly discovered the bitch within; taught it all the subtle airs and graces, refined and nurtured it, then let it out into the world with the precision and elegant accuracy of a master. Indeed, so perfected were her jabs and spars that to report the details here would seem inappropriate lest it mar the memory of a once-great artist or inspire entirely the wrong kind of behaviour amongst the younger generation of lady readers. Ever dutiful, Jamie sat quietly near the exit, patiently watching from a distance, appalled at what he was seeing. At one point drinks were thrown, though none of the liquid concerned reached its intended target. Then, finally, at around 1:15am, Madonna and her entourage left with Amanda following closely behind.

As the door to the outside world swung open they were greeted with a torrential hail of flashes. Amanda seized her moment, shouting at Madonna:

"You ******* ****! You'd **** your ****** for ********!! ****** ******** *****!!!" She was correctly assuming that words don't come out in photographs.

The insult hit its mark with all the pointed perfection of a bee-sting. Madonna reacted instinctively, swinging round and catching Amanda on the cheek with her fist. Amanda then responded by grabbing Madonna by the hair and the two engaged in a wrestling match during which Amanda somehow contrived to have her skirt ripped off. All the while they were screaming expletives at each other like angry chimpanzees. And then, as suddenly as it had started, it was over. Madonna was gone. Amanda suddenly became once again aware of the photographers and grabbed for her skirt, which was on the floor nearby. She was crying. She was happy. The cameras kept flashing.

The following Monday, at 11:04 am they were ushered into Filch's office.

"Ah, Manda, do come in. Splendid work. You've seen the papers I assume?" He was almost grinning, though it came across as more of a grimace, and the boil on his nose had vividly yellowed.

Amanda had indeed read the papers. She had read the articles over and over, and drank up the pictures as if they were the elixir of life itself. Generally they were sympathetic towards her in their portrayal of the "incident", but she didn't really care what they were saying so long as it was about her. That was all that really mattered.

Filch held up a spread from the *Boston Herald*. "MADGE MAULS MANDA!" the headline declared, and there were four pictures: the first showing Madonna's impressive right hook; the second and third of the pair of them locked in a vicious bear hug; and the last of Amanda, in tears, makeup streaked, trying to preserve what remained of her dignity whilst reaching down for her ripped off skirt.

"Oh yeah! It was fun," she replied, and her face became one large grin. She took the seat closest to the desk, whilst Jamie meekly sat in the other chair, which had been moved some distance away, by the wall.

"And you certainly picked the right girl. She was delighted. Even sent me a thank you card."

"What? She's a client of yours too?"

"Oh they're all my clients . . . Now! Next step. We have to move fast at this stage to build up momentum. Do you take any drugs?"

"No . . . well, other than the occasional bit of pot."

"Hmmm. That's not really . . . well we can keep it in reserve . . . Would you? Or pretend maybe? Would you care if the papers said you did?"

"Errr . . ."

"No. Wait. Got it. Perfect. The mystery just adds. We'll check you into the Betty Ford Clinic. Just for a few days. Not make any comment why. Let them speculate. I'll arrange your arrival for 2pm tomorrow. And don't worry, they won't treat you or anything. It'll be like a five star holiday . . . You'll love it. They'll love it. The paper's will love it. We'll all love it."

"So you work with them then? The Betty Ford Clinic?"

"No. Not with them. They're also clients. They have a suite set up for situations like this. It's good for them, it's good for you, it's good for me . . . we're all happy! . . . I'll call them now. And, naturally, let a few other people know too. See you next Monday then. Say midday . . . precisely, mind." And once again Filch turned towards the phone and the meeting was over. As they left, both Amanda and Jamie noted that he had seemed unusually jolly on this occasion. Amanda took this to be a sign that things were going particularly well. Jamie, on the other hand, was just a little bit suspicious. However, knowing what all this meant to Amanda he chose not to air his concerns.

The Betty Ford Clinic was indeed, as promised, much like a five star hotel. Her suite was luxurious, self-contained and in an entirely separate building from the treatment blocks, which was something of a relief as Amanda most definitely did not wish to mix with the "addicts". But most importantly, she had all the relevant papers and magazines delivered each morning, and thus spent much of the rest of the day lying on her bed drinking hot chocolate whilst flicking through the many pages, reading all about her stay and the various speculations that surrounded it; for in her brief period without publicity she had learnt to value it all the more. As Sunday evening loomed signalling the end of her stay, she displayed a clear reluctance to leave, only checking out at the very last minute. It had all been very refreshing; to be talked about without having to even do anything . . . Filch certainly seemed to know his business.

The next day, at precisely twelve o'clock, Amanda and Jamie were ushered once again into Filch's office.

"Ah, Jamie, dear Jamie . . . I have a little job for you." Jamie was somewhat surprised as this was the first time Filch had addressed him directly.

"Take this to the address on the front," and he held out a large padded envelope. "It's important . . . for Amanda."

Jamie looked at Amanda and her eyebrows said "do it", so he took the package and made for the door.

"Be quick mind. It's rather time sensitive."

Once Jamie had left Amanda noticed that there seemed to be

only one chair on her side of the desk. She turned her attention to Filch. His nose had swollen up to almost twice its usual size and his lip bristles were coated in what she hoped was cappuccino foam.

"What was that all about?" she asked, hastily returning her thoughts to Jamie, before her disgust at his appearance showed.

"Oh, just a little insurance policy, to see he plays ball . . . You're going to have to get of rid him you know. He has qualms, and in this business you can't afford to have qualms . . ." and he let out a little chuckle of self-satisfaction. "Right, so, where were we? . . . oh yes, how was Betty Ford? Good, I hope."

Amanda began excitedly gushing about her stay, though it was clear that Filch wasn't listening.

"Well, we certainly generated a great deal of speculation," Filch continued. "Now we deliver the payoff. The public does so love a fallen angel . . . the only question remains . . . what exactly is the nature of your fall?" He slowly chewed on the last sentence like a hard but delicious sweet toffee.

"Of course we can't give it all away at once . . . we need to keep them guessing, but throw them a few scraps from the high table, a little something to keep up their interest . . . You ever been in any trouble?"

"What kind of trouble?"

"You know, with the law."

"Not really. Got a few points on my license."

"Hmmm . . . tell me, are you really committed to this? . . . I mean, just how far are you prepared to go?"

"Oh, trust me, I'm committed. Fuck yeah!"

"Good. So you gotta get yourself arrested, right. Nothing too serious, but not too trivial either. Britney and Winona have already done the shoplifting thing, so it needs to be more than that. Naomi's kinda cornered the assault thing too, and that never really worked anyways; put people off her. Whatever, it needs to show a little vulnerability. Maybe get yourself a 51.50, you know, the psych ward. We need to make them think that you're losing it, make them sympathise..."

"... I could run naked round Times Square, that might be fun."

"No no no, that's a little too much . . . for now anyways," he chuckled to himself, obviously enjoying the image. "But I do like your thinking . . . hmmm . . . ok, how about this: a complete emotional breakdown whilst trying on lingerie at La Petite Coquette. I can see it now; wandering the store in tears, makeup smeared across your face shouting at random customers, cursing your figure, all in an unnecessary state of undress. If we're lucky we may get a shot of you sobbing your heart out, naked and vulnerable. Or even better; being dragged off by the police in your underwear. Yes, that really would be a coup. What do you think?"

"Sure, easy. Yeah."

"And if we can get you a 51.50, I'll get you into Elmira. I have friends there. It won't be as cushy as Betty Ford, but still, it could be a lot worse. And I've heard the food is great."

"Sure, yeah. Great."

"So shall we say Wednesday evening, La Petite Coquette?"

"Yeah, Wednesday's good."

"Oh, and don't mention anything to Jamie. I suspect he will disapprove, maybe cause problems . . . I think you should do it as soon as possible, getting rid of him that is. He has become surplus to your requirements, I do hope you can see that."

In all her excitement at the pending exhibitionism she had completely forgotten about Jamie. Yes, she could see it had to be done, but the sudden knot in her stomach reminded her that she had grown quite fond of him over the last few years. It would be a shame, but she knew what was important now, and she certainly wasn't going to throw away her chance for mere sentimentality.

On Wednesday evening Amanda gave the greatest performance of her life so far, rightly earning herself the required 51.50 for a stay at Elmira Psychiatric Centre, where she arrived at around midnight amid a veritable scrum of photographers so dense that security had to be called to clear a path for the ambulance through the main gate. The following morning's papers were everything she had hoped for, some photographs even making it onto the front pages of certain tabloids both in America and even across Europe. That was new. She hadn't hit the European papers for many months now, and though she knew Europe to be something of a backwater, it was still publicity: there were people across the pond reading about her, and wasn't that what "world famous" meant? Yes, things had gone spectacularly well.

As ever, Filch was right, about everything. The food was indeed pretty good, though the service was poor, and she hated the pale green they made her wear: it made her look shapeless, washed out, almost ill, like some kind of hospital patient. But it wouldn't be for long. No, her main concern now was dealing with Jamie. She knew he would show up sooner or later, probably sooner, and no doubt gushing with concern and sympathy, wanting to put things right. Ach, he could be so damned annoying! And she curled up in her hospital bed, flicking through the gossip channels, hoping to catch what they were saying about her, taking her mind off the impending scene between her and her oh-so-loyal assistant.

True to form, Jamie arrived five minutes into visiting hours bearing chocolates, flowers and a puppy-dog look of concern.

"Amanda, what happened? Are you ok?"

Amanda put on the most manipulatively vulnerable face she could muster.

"Oh Jamie, I'm so sorry."

"Don't be silly. You have nothing to be sorry about. But what happened? It wasn't another one of Filch's schemes was it?"

She didn't know what to say. She was so used to manipulating him, or so she thought, that her instinct was to be pitiable, weak and needy, but now wasn't the time for that. No she had to be tough. She pulled herself up on her bed.

"Jamie. I'm going to have to let you go."

"What?"

"You've become surplus to our requirements. I'm sorry. I'm

really so sorry, but that's that."

"What? You're firing me? I don't understand. Why?"

"Jamie my dear, you have qualms, and in this business you can't afford to have qualms."

"But Amanda . . . we have a history . . . you can't just fire me, I'm your friend."

"Jamie we're done. Didn't you hear? You're fired, that's it. We're done. Done, done, done!" and she gave him a steely cold look to underline the point. Though the discussion did in fact continue for a further five minutes, with many accusations and recriminations thrown on both sides, nothing further was actually communicated. When Jamie left, he had the look of a man whose heart had been most cruelly broken, and that was, in all likelihood, the case. Amanda just curled up again in the bed, as if nothing at all had happened, and continued flicking through the gossip channels. But something was different. Somewhere inside she knew she was now alone. And that was a good thing, right? No one to hold her back now.

* * * *

The following months continued in similar vein, with numerous ruses, counter-ruses, and cunning little schemes expertly devised by Filch and extravagantly executed by Amanda. There was a staged on-off relationship with WWF wrestler Hell's Hammer; a much publicised arrest for possession of illegally imported Chinese medicines, amongst them a dried tiger's penis and mummified panda paw (Amanda personally found these items to be rather disgusting, but kept them in her bag in the hope that they might be discovered at an opportune moment, as indeed they were); various catfights with other publicity hungry "celebrities", each of them among Filch's many desperate clients; a carefully contrived impatience with the photographers, ultimately resulting in a number of charges being levelled against her for assault and destruction of property; and many more, too numerous to mention here. Amanda took to wearing thicker, more excessive theatrical makeup, even whilst in bed, that her features might be clearly defined in the craftiest of long distance shots. Indeed she became so enamoured with "the game" that six months passed before she realised she hadn't sat at her keyboard or sung a single note since her first meeting with Filch. And so, the following Monday, as she sat in the expensive chair, waiting for Filch to get off the phone, she decided to suggest maybe doing a few gigs again. Finally he clamped the receiver down on its base, as if seeking dramatic effect, and swung around on his chair to face Amanda. He had clearly had some kind of operation as his nose was completely covered with an excessively large dressing stained in yellow, red and brown, and his moustache had been trimmed, presumably to attach the dressing, so that only the tips remained giving the appearance of two large hairy moles on either side of his mouth. Amanda gulped quietly to herself and blurted out,

"I've been thinking of putting on a show."

Filch looked momentarily horrified, before what was left of his face relaxed into a smile, then a grin, and finally erupted into laughter. "Manda, Manda, Manda. You leave the ideas to me."

"No, I'm serious. I mean, I'm supposed to be a musician, aren't I?"

Filch leant forward across his desk, and gave her his most serious look. "Listen. Sure, when you first came to me you were a musician, and where was that getting you? Your publicity capital was plummeting. Nobody gave a damn. Sure you could have struggled on, playing ever smaller venues until . . . well let's just say it wouldn't have lasted long. Now, today, you're a superstar, one of the most talked about girls in the whole of the US. And, to be frank, it's got fuck all to do with music."

"But my fans will want to see me play."

"Take my word for it, your fans are far more interested in what you're wearing, and who you're bitching about than hearing you sing. There are a million perfectly good singers out there, but only a handful of superstars. It would be a huge step backwards."

"But can't I be a superstar *and* a singer?"

"Hmmmm . . ." Filch leant far back on his chair and looked up at the ceiling. "Hmmm" he said again turning his gaze back to her. "Well . . . ok, so here's what we can do: I'll ask around, get you a good slot at some big event, maybe the Central Park Summerstage, or some such. But, and this is important, you have to play the role. Remember, you're a train wreck, and America loves a train wreck. If you go out there and put on a good show all our work will be undone . . . Do you drink? Yes, course you do. So drink a bottle of bourbon before you go on, or fake it if you can. Fall off the stage, swear at the audience, forget your words, lay into the band, whatever, but make it a disaster. Trust me, Manda, if you want to sing it's the only way not to fuck it all up"

"Sure, I can do that." There was obviously a hint of reservation in her tone as Filch gave her his serious look again.

"You're not having any qualms are you, because..."

"I know, I know. In this business there's no room for qualms."

It turned out that the Summerstage was entirely booked up, and even Filch, with all of his many contacts and favours owed, was unable, or perhaps unwilling, to find a slot for Amanda at such short notice. But she was not herself without contacts and independently bagged a headlining spot at Chicago's Lollapalooza Festival later that month. Indeed, the promoters were so enthusiastic that not only had they offered her a sizeable fee, but also the use of the house band, which included many of Chicago's top session musicians, a number of whom she had performed with in the past. Amanda was very excited at the prospect. Over the past year she had forgotten how much she loved performing; the glare of the lights, the roar of the fans, oh yes, it felt good to be back on track. And now she was a superstar it could only be better than ever. She had three weeks to get herself back on form, and, despite her promise to Filch, she felt it couldn't hurt to at least do herself justice at the sound-check.

The three weeks passed like no time at all with Amanda uncharacteristically withdrawn from the public eye, she was so absorbed in her practice. Not that that put off the photographers, who perpetually lurked behind bushes and parked cars with their telephoto lenses aimed not so discretely at her balcony. And it was always a refreshing break for her to indulge in a little faux-naive exhibitionism between songs. Oh yes, things had never been better; she was at the very pinnacle of her career, and it felt so good.

The morning of the show found Amanda swanning around backstage as if the whole great event had been set up just for her. She had flown into Chicago two days earlier to ensure she was fully refreshed and on top form. And, of course, to give the media, and other bands, plenty of opportunity to notice she was there. Naturally the VIP area wasn't quite so luxurious as what she was used to, having been set up in an otherwise public park, but her trailer had been done out nicely with colourful Turkish draperies, and all the many specifications of her rider had been well-catered for: white lilies and black roses, bowls of fresh fruit, a fridge stocked with champagne and orange juice, and an excessively large bowl filled with her favourite European hand-made chocolates. Although, in truth, she had little interest in hiding behind the trailer's closed doors, oh no, she wanted to be seen, to bathe in the glory of her headlining position. And deep within her bag lay the bottle of Jack Daniels Filch had given her with much emphasis at the airport, to lubricate the necessary forthcoming disaster.

She hadn't paid much attention to the array of acts supporting her, and was mildly disappointed to find that a fair number of them were newcomers whom she had barely heard of: the Nifty Spinsters, B-side, Jonah's Whale, Professor Zitch, Bonfire Madigan, Miranda Barker; who were these guys? But then that was the nature of such events. She was, after all, the mast to which they were pinning their colours in the hope of future attention. And why not? Fifteen years ago she had been amongst them herself, desperate to get noticed by hanging onto the coat-tails of various stars of the day, many of whom were now long forgotten, although some had made it through to become today's venerated elder statesmen of the industry, as she knew she would in years to come. Oh yes, today would be a good day.

The sound-check was little more than a walk-on walk-off affair, giving her barely time enough to run through a single chorus, although she did receive a fair few cheers from the many musicians and performers nervously milling around awaiting their own turn. Once she was done she joined the throng to lap up whatever praise was on offer before retiring to her trailer. This was the bit she had always disliked – sitting around, waiting for her moment: hell, she had six hours to kill, and that was if things were running to schedule, which they never were. It was the first time she had done this alone, and she had to admit she did miss Jamie, despite his qualms. She picked at the chocolates, considered doing some yoga, and then decided to take a little nap.

Five hours later she was in full costume and had added an additional layer to her richly caked makeup. She was sat, cross-legged on the plush sheepskin rug provided in her rider, eyeing up the bottle of Jack Daniels. She pulled the cork and took a big gulp, then placed it back on the floor in front of her. As the warmth coursed through her body she considered what she was doing. Certainly Filch had been right about many things: he had after all made her a bigger star than she could have ever managed on her own; hell, she was one of the most talked about singers in the whole of America, maybe even the world. Before it had been about her music, and that had got her pretty far, but now it was about her, and how she loved the attention; but this was a great event to be playing, and it felt wrong to screw it up, whatever Filch thought he knew. And anyway, hadn't she always put on a good show? Wasn't that how she had made her name in the first place? She took another great gulp, only this time in went down the wrong way, resulting in a most undignified coughing fit. Was that a sign? Was the whiskey saying don't do it? She could feel the pride rising in her belly. No! She wouldn't do it. Filch may know about PR, but he had no interest in art. And she was after all an artist! She took the bottle and poured it down the sink. She was going to go out there and do what she had always done: put on the best show she could. She was

Amanda Palmer, singer and songwriter par excellence. She would show them all!

* * * *

The next morning she woke early in her hotel bed and urgently rang room service to enquire if the newspapers had been delivered yet. It was an impatient half an hour before a thick wad of papers arrived at her room which she received with great enthusiasm, tipping the porter a full hundred dollars. But as she hurried through them it quickly became apparent that there was nothing; not a single mention of the festival, and more importantly, not a single mention of her. But then the gig had been late last night. Maybe they just hadn't got anything to press on time. Probably tomorrow. And so she spent a miserable day shopping in the fashionable end of Chicago, trying on dresses, shoes and bags before catching her flight back to New York later that evening.

The following morning's papers had a number of reviews of the festival but to her horror she was barely mentioned. "Miranda Barker Steals the Show" was the headline on page three of the *New York Times* arts pages. The article merely referred to Amanda in passing: "Amanda Palmer gave an adequate performance but there was no sign of the sparkling effervescence and sexy panache she once displayed." The other papers followed suit with photographs of Miranda Barker, and little if any mention of Amanda. Who the hell was this Miranda Barker character anyway? Amanda tried calling Filch repeatedly, but his secretary claimed he was out, or unavailable. Finally, at around five o'clock that afternoon her phone rang.

"Hello, Miss Palmer. Filch here. I believe you called."

She hadn't thought through what she was planning to say to him and found herself somewhat tongue-tied, but it seemed that Filch was in no mood for listening anyway and he barely waited for her response before continuing.

"I must say I am very disappointed in you Miss Palmer, and

surprised. I thought we had an understanding. I'd invested a lot of time in you. What were you thinking?"

"I just wanted to put on a good show. That's what I do. Surely it's not so bad. It was just one show."

"I'm afraid it's too late now Miss Palmer. You're time was already over when you came to me, and as I explained to you at the beginning, I may be able to manipulate these things, but I cannot turn the tide. And without your cooperation . . . You were riding a wave, Miss Palmer, your last wave, and you see, you've fallen off the board. The only thing left to do now is sink, and preferably with some dignity."

In desperation Amanda continued with the maritime imagery. "But it was just one show . . . Surely I can climb back onto the board? Find something to hang onto? Can't you throw me some oars?"

"Sure I could throw you some oars, but without a boat you would still sink. Even the gulls have stopped circling. You're out of fish and they know it."

"But it can't be over. It was all going so well. For fuck's sake, it was just one show . . ."

"To be honest, Miss Palmer, it wasn't just one show. It was bound to end soon enough anyways. Frankly I was surprised we kept it all going for as long as we did."

"But . . ."

"No, Miss Palmer. It's over. We're done."

"But . . ."

"We're done."

"But . . ."

"We're Done! I wish you luck in your future ventures," and he hung up the phone.

So many emotions were welling up inside her she didn't know what it was she felt. There was anger, frustration, shame, desperation, panic, loss, even grief. All she could do was let out the loudest, most monstrous scream of her life and then smash up much of her furniture. If only Jamie were here. He'd know what to do.

He'd sort it all out. After fifteen minutes of violence she lay on the bed sobbing, and reached for the phone.

"Jamie?" Her voice was barely audible through the tears.

"Who's that?"

"Jamie, it's me, Amanda."

"Oh . . . Hi Amanda. How's tricks."

"Jamie, I want you back, I need you."

There was a long pause. "But Amanda, you dumped me." His voice sounded cold, indifferent. Not like Jamie.

"It was all a mistake. The biggest mistake of my life. Please..."

"I'm sorry Amanda. I've moved on. You forced me to move on. I'm working for Miranda Barker now."

"Who the fuck is that bitch!" Another long pause.

"I think I should go now. Please, don't call me again." And with that he hung up. This time she didn't have the energy for another tantrum, and so just lay in bed, quietly weeping until finally sleep took her briefly from her misery.

Over the following weeks Amanda shrank to a shadow of her former self. She didn't wash, and barely ate, spending her time vacantly staring at her TV screen, or wandering the streets of Manhattan in a daze, scaring passing children as the various peeling layers of her makeup gave her something of the appearance of a Hollywood zombie. And she did indeed feel like the living dead. After all, if a star is never photographed can she still be a star? If a singer sings to an empty hall, does she make a sound? And if no longer a star, or even a singer come to that, then what was she? She had never been a normal person, a member of the audience classes. It was as if everything that made her Amanda had been stripped away, leaving what? Was there anything left underneath it all? Such were the thoughts whirring around her head as she placed one foot in front of the other in no particular direction. And there, at every newspaper kiosk and magazine stand was her nemesis staring back at her: Miranda Barker—My Secrets for Looking Good; Get Fit With Miranda; Miranda's Top Tips for a Better Love Life; Sex, Boys and Macrobiotics—Miranda Bares All;

hell, some magazines had even starting calling her Manda!

Then, one evening, Amanda decided it was time to wash the past from her by now emaciated soul, and so she ran herself a hot bath. As she lay there soaking in the deep water, gently wiping away the glamour and the makeup it became apparent that her greatest fear was indeed entirely justified; for with each touch of the sponge she seemed to fade, just a little, until finally nothing at all remained. It was as if she had dissolved in the water.

Six weeks later a neighbour alerted the police that something may be amiss at her apartment, for the lights had been left on, the curtains left open and the radio left playing. When the door was broken in and the apartment was searched they found her discarded clothes beside a full bath of water stained with many bright colours and no sign whatever of her body.

I would say that nothing was heard from her again, but rumour has it that on certain nights a disembodied voice can be heard quietly echoing around the apartment, and if you listen carefully you might just catch the words to her last hit song, *"(What's) the point of it all?"*; although, of course, it may just be a trick of the wind, quietly singing to itself amidst the telegraph wires.

A Personal Extroduction from Text Number Seven

By ███████████████

As soon as I read this story I knew I had found my choice, though I did dutifully read the many other hundreds of texts I was given, just to be sure. And, if I am honest, I was almost relieved that there were no other serious contenders, for I really wouldn't have wanted to put this rollicking tale to one side, as by then I had grown rather attached to it. Why? Well, largely because it was a story I recognised, on one level or another, from so many artists and bands I have worked with over the years, who lost their vision in the face of the great publicity machine. It is an age-old tale, doomed to be repeated for eternity, or for as long a mankind can muster the will to be.

Certainly this text is a satire, and a rather flat one at that. The characters are little more than two-dimensional ciphers, there to represent ideas rather than to live and breathe as themselves, mere crude stereotypes. But then stereotypes are just that for a reason. I mean who hasn't had a Filtch in their life? Or a Jamie? I know I have, repeatedly, and still I never see them coming. Thus, like all good satires, it holds a mirror to ourselves, revealing from a distance all the absurdities and contradictions that rule our lives, each and every one of us.

From a literary perspective it is not a particularly impressive piece, and is certainly far from the true spirit of the *palmeresque*. However it does have a certain charm, the occasional witty phrase, and is, once or twice, almost insightful. Basically it is a retelling of the Doctor Faustus story, and as such attempts the challenging task of becoming a modern morality tale about over-reaching ambition, perhaps a vice the story itself could be accused of. But despite its many failings I did find it most enjoyable and strangely comforting.

And I must admit I did smile at the portrayal of Amanda as a publicity whore. Had the Amanda I knew turned her prodigious talents towards mastering the publicity machine she would, without doubt, be more famous than Jesus. Thankfully, for all of us, she stuck with writing songs to the end.

TEXT NUMBER EIGHT

On the Exultant Death of Amanda Palmer

It was unusually warm that morning, as it had been for nearly a week now, possibly due to the thick blanket of cloud that had sat upon the moors since the New Year. This had been a cause of much debate amongst the shepherds at the Goat and Firkin, the only drinking establishment in that corner of the North Moor, as it made the job of tending the flocks so much harder. Joseph Grimble was missing ten sheep somewhere south of Crow Tor and rumours were rife that the beast was abroad. Strange moans had been heard drifting on the wind near Wistman's Wood where the Devil was said to drive his hounds, and Grimble was reluctant to venture too deep into the valley. Still if the sheep were not found he would lose nearly a month's wages, and he feared his wife more than rumours, for her savage tongue put the Devil to shame. So that morning he had left his son in charge of the flock and headed south towards the Tor. In his pocket were his grandfather's crucifix and the *Book of Common Prayer*, just in case. He did not consider himself a superstitious man, but even so, out on the moors, in the mist, in the very deep of winter, well the mind can play tricks on even the most rational of men.

Two hours later he stood atop of Crow Tor, scouring the landscape with the short telescope he had purchased the previous spring, for his eyes were not what they used to be. There was no sign of his sheep on the higher ground, and the mist that filled the valleys obscured any notion of an easy resolution, but as he hopped from the great rock with surprising agility for a man of his age, he came upon a trail of droppings that filled him both with hope and a little dread, for they led him down the slope into the mist towards Wistman's Wood, an ancient fairy wood, ripe with myth and legend, and generally avoided by all who had but an ounce of common sense.

It was heavy going as there was no path and the steep hillside was densely strewn with granite boulders, each one dressed with moss, and made all the more treacherous in this dreadful damp. One false step and his ankle would snap like a stick. He could see but twenty feet ahead of him, and when the first gnarly oak loomed through the mist he caught himself muttering the Lord's Prayer. "Now don't be a fool, Joseph," he thought, but finished the prayer nonetheless. He had left Night, his jet-black border collie, with his son, and now began to regret it. Night was afraid of nothing, and his courage was infectious. He would take on creatures twice his size and rarely came away with even a scratch. But he was needed to guard the flock, what with rumours of the beast being abroad, and anyway, Grimble was known for his sturdiness of heart and devoutness of spirit: he had his reputation to consider; if ever a man had God on his side it was he. As a youth he had become something of a local hero when the church caught fire and he had risked life and limb to rescue the bones of St. Boniface. For that he had received a commendation from the Bishop, and a silver spoon, now long since lost. Yet age has a way of withering resolve and fear and superstition seeps in through the cracks. Legends, he thought, don't just spring from the air, and this place, this fairy wood, was rife with them. He had heard the tales as a child, and oft repeated them as a father.

Grimble made his way forward toward the tree line, and then stopped again and sat himself down upon a cushion of damp moss. No point in facing the Devil on an empty stomach, he thought, and took from his coat pocket a brown paper parcel tied in rough string, which he proceeded to unwrap. It was a salted mutton and turnip pasty, not his favourite but tasty enough, and all the better washed down with strong liquor: he always kept his flask filled with Brown's "whiskey". No one knew what Brown put in that stuff but it certainly packed a punch and kept out the cold. By now the sun was high and the mist was beginning to clear, though it seemed to linger still among the twisted shapes ahead of him. He hesitated a moment longer to consider what he might find within. There was no doubt about it. His sheep had wandered into the wood, probably seeking shelter from the wind, and he would have to follow. And surely neither the devil nor the fairies would take any great interest in sheep; after all did not the Bible state that they had no soul? In truth he had always puzzled over this, as they seemed to have their own personalities, but Father Stringer was a wise enough man to know such things, and so Grimble chose to take his word, for though he knew much about sheep he knew little about the workings of the soul. Fortified in body, if not spirit, he clenched his heart and headed into the wood.

There was something unaccountably ancient about this place, even the air tasted stale and musty, and the trees, bent and twisted like crooked old witches draped in beggar's rags: he felt like a tres-passer venturing into some nether-world that should not be dis-turbed. The ground was densely strewn with moss-covered rocks and mouldering vegetation fed upon by strangely coloured fungus growths the like of which he had not seen before. Every branch hung with fronds of lichen, some as long as an arm, that brushed at his face as he willed his way slowly forward. The silence was unnerving, and he made every effort to make his own stumbling progress as quiet as was possible, as if for fear of waking some-thing unknown, unknowable, and best left at rest. Occasionally this silence was broken by the scuttling of tiny claws upon the rocks and once he came upon an adder which quickly slithered out of sight at his approach. Though the wood was not big, its density and uneven sloping contours meant that the search would have to be particularly thorough, and was taking much longer than he had hoped: certainly he wanted to be well away before dusk.

One, maybe two hours passed and he had started rehearsing reports of his failure to his wife when he heard something large moving not too far ahead. He stopped. There it was again. Certainly a large animal, possibly a number of them, and a chill ran through him. It was either his sheep, or the Devil's Wish Hounds were beginning to stir. His instinct was to hide and wait, but duty sent him creeping tentatively towards the sound. Then, as if out of nowhere, a bleat, and the feeling of relief nearly knocked him over. He almost forgot where he was and strode confidently forward towards what turned out to be a small clearing. There were three, four, no six of his sheep sat contentedly on the mossy ground, chewing away, and as he entered the clearing he could see two more between the trees a little further up the hillside. No doubt the others were nearby. They looked up casually and seemed to recognise him, before returning to their chewing. Grimble sat down upon a rock not more than a yard away and took the flask from his pocket as if to congratulate himself. But as he drank he heard something else, something that sent a shiver right through him, something like a moan but not quite human, and it seemed to be very close, and coming from behind him. He jumped up, spun around, and there before him, not more than six yards away, was the most appalling sight he had ever seen. At first he thought it must be some spirit apparition, some ghastly ghoul risen from hell itself to torment his soul, but then he realised it was all too real, and a deep terror and dread gripped his soul the like of which he had never felt before. His body shook uncontrollably and before he could think he was on his knees, heaving up the contents of his stomach and mouthing prayers between the bursts of bile and mutton. Once he had regained control over his body he looked again: it was a woman, or rather the wrecked shell of a woman, little more than a girl, nailed to the remnants of a rotting stump in a savage mockery of the crucifixion. This was no sanitised image of spiritual suffering; it was a violent and bloody sight; just to look upon the pain-racked face seemed an unbearable torture to him. And then it hit him that this body, this shell of a girl was still alive, barely, and he realised that he had to do something: but what to do? Her wrists were pierced with massive nails, like those used to secure railway sleepers, as were her feet, and he had no idea how to go about removing them, or even if he should. And there was so much blood. Her clothes, strange clothes, a tarts clothes the like of which he had never seen before, were entirely soaked through, though the bleeding itself seemed to have stopped as the blood was congealed and glooped around her wrists like wax running down the stem of a candle. Grimble just stood and stared, completely baffled as to how to proceed until another dull moan shook him from this ghastly reverie and the urgency of action hit him. He moved towards the girl and tentatively pulled at one of the nails. There was no way he could do this alone. He would have to get help, and quickly. He wanted to speak, to console her somehow, but the words wouldn't come, and so he turned and ran towards the nearest farm house up by Two Bridges, not more than a mile away. He would get help. He would get Father Stringer, yes, the good Father would know what should be done.

* * * *

The strange procession slowly wound its way along the misty musty moorland footpaths like a scene from some medieval painting. At its head was Father Stringer, a man whose enormous force of personality was larger even than his immense form, or indeed his vastly oversized moustache. At his side walked Grimble, pale and uncertain by comparison, and behind them trailed most of the local congregation, for despite the distance between the various ragged farms, houses and workshops that made up the parish of Two Bridges, it was a tight little community, and when something untoward occurred word would get around with unfathomable speed. This part of the moors had never ventured into the modern world; there were no telegraph poles, no mobile phone masts, and even the roads themselves were barely more than dirt tracks. And that was the way they all wanted it to stay, for who would live in such an anachronistic backwater if not by choice? Most of them rarely ventured beyond the boundaries of the moor itself, not if they could help it, for the world beyond seemed alarmingly chaotic and cruel. Father Stringer had lived, for a time, in the local city of Exeter. It was there that he had attended the seminary that had polished his vocation and made him a priest, but he had been all too happy to return to the peace and stillness of his youth. Nowadays he took no interest in anything outside this quiet little empire of souls. Indeed he resented any intrusions, and by all accounts at this moment they were heading towards just such an intrusion.

As they approached the edge of Wistman's Wood an anxious hush descended upon the assembled crowd, and their pace began to waver. Only Father Stringer retained his determination, as he headed, unperturbed, into the damp and gloomy tree-line, shouting behind him various words of encouragement and holy invocations to urge his followers onwards. At the back of the ragged crowd Mary-Beth clutched tightly to her grandmother's bony hand. Her parents had both died when she was six and now it was her grandmother who looked after the awkward and gangly eleven-year-old girl. She had never been a problem, was always polite and did her chores without arguing, but nonetheless Granny Rowther greatly resented this imposition upon her dotage. Certainly she was a tough old bird; she still baked her own bread, kept up her own vegetable garden, and every morning walked the five miles to Tavistock post-office to drink tea with the Blakeneys and catch up on all the local gossip. No, it was not so much the effort but the responsibility she begrudged. She had disliked being a mother the first time around and had little patience for this second run, and so, with callous indifference she pulled her hand away, and moved forward to talk to Widower Shrive, for whom, as everyone knew, she had something of a liking. Mary-Beth was used to such rejections, but still on this occasion, what with the woods and the rumours, it stung her a little more than usual. She had learnt to be brave over the past five years, so took a deep breath and followed the others, counting to ten over and over in her head like her mother had taught her.

The little wood was damper than the day before and the air smelt ripe with rotting mulch and fungus. Everywhere water dripped from the leafless branches and trailing lichens, and occasional glimpses of sunlight sparkled here and there, trapped within the droplets like tiny precious gemstones. The mist was clearing, lending the wood a slightly brighter magical feel, though not without an air of lingering menace. Mary-Beth could hear the resonant tone of Father Stringer rumbling on in the distance, but chose to focus instead on the tuneful chirrup of the skylarks above the trees, and the gentle pitter-patter of water falling upon granite at her feet.

Suddenly her wilful reverie was broken by a wild hubbub up ahead. Shouts, gasps and exclamations burst through the wood sending her heart racing with fear, and she ran to catch up with the others. Once they were back in sight her pace slowed just a little. Then, just as suddenly as it had begun, the crowd was silenced by the booming voice of Father Stringer. There they were, clustered in a small clearing. It seemed that they were gathered around something, though what it was she couldn't see, for she was still quite small for her age. The good Father Stringer was holding forth with more vigour and passion than she had heard in him before. There was a strange tone to his voice, an excitement, though she couldn't quite catch the words. Now back amongst the reassuring crowd her fear turned to curiosity and she carefully sewed her way through the mass of bodies to the front, but before she could reach her destination she felt someone grab her by the shoulder and turn her round. It was Widower Shrive, white as a sheet, a look of shock and horror in his eyes.

"You mustn't look my dear. It's too... too dreadful." But she shook him off and pushed her way through.

There, standing upon a large granite boulder, was Father Stringer, preaching with an intensity that none had heard from him before: "... Behold! Behold the Hand of God in action. This gift, a gift to us, a sign to us alone that we have not been forgotten. That He has sent this sign to us is proof if ever proof were needed that all our ministries and Faith have been heard, and have been listened to: that the turning of our backs upon the many innumerable sins that wreak their daily havoc upon the souls of all who have embraced the modern world, its ease of sin, its open ear toward the devil's work, has this day been rewarded. For here, behold: the Love of God. For did He not Love his only son, and yet He sent him to be nailed upon the cross, for Love of us, his flock. And here, today, we see His Love in action once again. This pitiable girl, this harlot, strumpet, tart, this evil vessel, who no doubt plied her sinful trade amongst the Devil's city lights, He has plucked from the path of her Soul's destruction, and granted her the gift of Love, His Love, His ultimate forgiveness. And though today, before us all, she wears the visage of pain and suffering, yet still it is surely as nothing to the pain and suffering that her soul no doubt endured before this act of Love; it is as surely as nothing to the suffering and eternal torment He has saved her from, were she left to burn amidst the agonising flames of Hell's fire and brimstone. Behold! . . . "

Mary-Beth was so entranced by the unfamiliar passion in the good Father's voice that she did not at first notice the girl who was the object of his sermonising; but then her eyes followed his vigorous gesturing towards the pitiable figure and his voice seemed to fade into the distance. She was so beautiful, that young woman, despite the wounds and her pained expression. Mary-Beth had never seen such beauty, not in real life; like the girls in the magazine she had once found at the roadside, that her grandmother had called "filth" and thrown onto the fire. And her clothes were unlike anything Mary-Beth had ever come upon before, ever even imagined: long stockings striped in black and white, and a small silky black top, so thin that the generous curves of her body were clearly visible beneath. Was this how her own body would grow? The only female form she had ever seen undressed was her grandmother, but this girl, this young woman: she yearned to reach out to her, to touch her, to trace those richly ripened curves with her fingers.

".. . and so let us pray. Let us pray with more vigour and in greater earnest that ever have we prayed before! For here, here where we now stand, in this sacred grove He did walk . . . here amongst us has He revealed his infinite might . . . Let us fall to our knees, fall to our knees and bow our hearts in deep humility . . ."

As the makeshift congregation fell to its knees Mary-Beth was roused from her fantasy and quickly followed suit, mouthing the familiar words as she continued to stare at the twisted body.

"Our Father, who art in heaven, hallowed be thy name. Thy Kingdom come, thy will be done, on earth as it is in heaven. Give us this day our daily bread. And forgive us our trespasses, as we forgive those who trespass against us. And lead us not into temptation, but deliver us from evil. For thine is the kingdom, the power and the glory. Forever and ever. Amen."

"Now let us sing Hymn number 167, *Lamb of God.*"

"Lamb of God, for sinners slain, To thee I feebly pray; Heal me of my grief and pain, O take my sins away! From this bondage, Lord, release, No longer let me be opprest; Jesus, Master, seal my peace, And take me to thy breast! . . ."

As their massed voices echoed around the eerie wood each note took on a strange other-worldly quality. Rabbits and mice were startled, and scurried back to their borrows; birds flocked to the air and circled above, confused by the unfamiliar sounds; snakes slithered out of view; even the clouds of midges seemed to vanish in the breeze.

". . . Let it not, my Lord, displease that I would die to be thy guest. Jesus, Master, seal my peace, and take me to thy breast!"

The silence that followed seemed suddenly deeper and darker than ever before. Father Stringer had never felt so powerful, so truly in the service of the Lord: God was almost upon him, He was at his ear, whispering divinely; and his disciples were in complete abeyance. It was as if the previous twenty-five years of his ministry had each day been carefully laying the foundations for this single moment. He took a little time to let it all sink within before continuing:

"And so, dear brethren, the time has come for us to leave this sacred place, to return to our homes and to meditate upon the IMMENSITY of IMPORT that this miracle has brought to our humble community. Tomorrow, at dawn, we shall meet at the church and hold a service of gratitude for what has happened here today. And then, once prayers have been said, confessions taken and humility regained, let us return to this place and build, around this very hallowed grove, a chapel, a humble church of wood, to honour and celebrate the redemption of this unknown sinner . . . Now let us sing Hymn number 143; *A Charge to Keep I Have*!" And the massed voices rang about the wood once again, only this time with more vehemence and commitment:

"A charge to keep I have. A God to glorify. A never-dying soul to save, and fit it for the sky; to serve the present age, my calling to fulfil: O may it all my powers engage To do my Master's will! . . ." At the end of this first verse Father Stringer stood down from the rock and, still singing with all his might, led the way back up the path and out of the wood, towards home. ". . . Arm me with jealous care, as in thy sight to live; and o thy servant, Lord, prepare a strict account to give! Help me to watch and pray, and on thyself rely; assured, if I my trust betray, I shall for ever die . . ."

Mary-Beth waited until the voices were little more than a distant rumble upon the wind before she ventured out from beneath a large granite slab that had at some point become dislodged and toppled by the ancient tree-roots, creating a neat little hidey-hole. She hadn't been ready to leave, and she knew she wouldn't be missed for many hours yet. She was fascinated by the girl; she pitied her, wanted to comfort her, somehow ease her pain. She tore a strip from the bottom of her petticoat and soaked it like a sponge in one of the many little pools amongst the rocks and trunks; then tentatively made her way toward the twisted figure. She really was very beautiful. Her face was white as a porcelain doll, topped with short-ish curly brown hair with just a hint of red. Her eyes were closed and her eyebrows seemed to be drawn on with some extravagance, like words from a book of spells. She was still breathing, but barely, and every now and then let out a shallow gasp. Mary-Beth reached forward and wiped the wet cloth gently against her face; she squeezed it just a little over the girl's scarlet painted lips, allowing water to flow into her mouth, but received no response. Then she carefully wiped away a small blotch of blood from the left corner of the girl's mouth, and watched a thin trickle of red-stained water run over her chin, down her neck, pooling at her collar bone before once again overflowing, running down her sternum, under her top, between her breasts. Mary-Beth moved a little closer, her heart was beating fast.

Amanda Palmer (for that had been her name) felt the gentle warmth of soft kisses upon her cheeks and finally slipped from this world to the next.

A Personal Extroduction from Text Number Eight

By ███████████████

I must confess I was initially surprised that crucifixion was such a common theme amongst the many texts I read: of the eight hundred and twenty-seven pieces, forty-two contained some form of crucifixion scene, of which eighteen were self-crucifixions. However after some musings on the subject, and discussions with various colleagues I came to realise that this is only to be expected, after all, which fan doesn't like to think of their dead hero as a martyr, and what easier way to express such a notion? Nonetheless I did find the gruesomeness of this approach toward portraying Amanda's death both fascinating and tantalising, and therefore decided to make my choice from this subject category.

So why this particular piece? After all, by my understanding it isn't even a real *palmeresque*, at least according to the generally accepted definition. Well, most of all I think it is the context of the crucifixion that caught my imagination, or rather the lack of context, for it is given no explanation whatsoever: Amanda's body is merely found nailed to a tree, in a remote English wood, by a superstitious shepherd whose community seems centuries out of time. The author offers no opinion or comment as to why or how, leaving something of an appetising flavour of mystery in the reader's mouth. What follows is a simplistic, yet entertainingly cruel, representation of the world's relationship with Amanda – to the older generation and the establishment, represented by Father Stringer, she symbolises all that is corrupt, debased and decadent in the modern world; to the young and repressed, represented by Mary-Beth, she is an object of sexual fascination. It is also worth noting that only the superstitious simpleton considers trying to take her down, everyone else has a vested interest in keeping her nailed up there for their own ends: Father Stringer and his congregation want to make her the centrepiece of a new church; Mary-Beth wants to discover her own sexuality by exploring/exploiting Amanda's body. The final scene, a clear biblical reference to Mary Magdalene, is beautifully presented and leaves the reader vividly imagining what happens next.

It is clearly a very confidently written piece, both in terms of what is included and what is left out. The descriptions are perfectly pointed, uneasy and luxurious, and the symbolism doesn't overly weigh upon the storyline.

I also noticed the cunning use of point-of-view. The work is divided into four sections, starting from Grimble's perspective, then moving through Father Stringer and Mary-Beth to finally arrive with Amanda as she dies upon the cross. In addition each section is made shorter than the last to give the piece a feeling of momentum.

Overall I found this to be a thoroughly entertaining and enjoyable read, although I might add that the preaching got a bit tedious towards the end.

In addition it may, or may not, be worth mentioning that the author is clearly unschooled in the biological realities of the Dartmoor environment, as a number of the creatures he/she mentions would be hibernating throughout the winter period during which the story is set.

TEXT NUMBER NINE

A Personal Extroduction from Text Number Nine

By ███████████

When I first came upon this text I was in no doubt that I had stumbled on something exceptional, extraordinary, a truly remarkable piece of writing, indeed it was in the hope of discoveries like this that the *palmeresque* project was first developed. The technical mastery is impressive in itself: effortlessly slipping from prose to verse, stream-of-consciousness to didactic debate; the imaginative delivery of past, present and future tenses; the complex integration and juxtaposition of multiple points of view; and of course the highly expressive use of footnotes. However, it is the content itself that really impresses: the vividness of description; the author's uncanny ability to place the reader inside the head of all the major protagonists simultaneously; and the seemingly effortless mastery of Gnostic symbolism, my personal favourite form of symbolism.

The narrative itself gently draws the reader into ███████

████████████████████████████████████
████████████████████████████████████
████████████████████████████████████
████████████████████████████████████
████████████████████████████████████
████████████████████████████████████
████████████████████████████████████
████████████████████████████████████
████████████████████████████████████
████████████████████████████████████
████████████████████████████████████

Overall, therefore, a magnificent effort, well worthy of its place in this, or indeed any, book.

TEXT NUMBER TEN

Upon the Death of Amanda Palmer

Some said she came across the mountains, riding bareback on a
battered nag and as it died it sighed and turned away
its head

Some said she crawled out from the ashes where Hildegard the
witch was burned: her face smeared with sultry attitude, her hair charred vivid red

Some said it was the sea that brought her, drowned, naked, strung
with pearls and glistening; a baby in her arms, smiling
like a fool

Some said she sprang up from the bishop's grave to lap at the
moon's reflection upon half-remembered icy pools

Some said she suckled bats in the forest: she sang them to sleep at
the edge of dawn, whilst the sun gently kissed her slender hand

Some said she had snuck in silently; wasted and defiled, betrayed;
a fine disguise amongst the many idle damned...

Her rich embrace: warm as a mother's breast, cool as polished ice,
enviable, much desired... Miraculous!

Some said the turn came willingly, dressed up to the nines, ineffa-
bly charming, and just a little bit effete

Some said that day turned to night and night turned to day, and
everything turned all about upon a tupenny piece

Some said it was the tide that had turned; a great wave of joy become shame that knocked her from foundation's grasp

Some said it wasn't yet her turn at all; that Accident and Fate were
playing dice—it seems her name came up by chance

Some said it turned on a vicious end, hissing and snarling, injured,
bitter and denied

Some said the turn came suddenly, leaping without warning from
a sickly blackening sky

They found her scurrying in churchyards: burning human hearts,
a girl with wings . . . Miraculous!

Some said her death had been there all along; palely considering,
voyeuristic, ever walking in her footsteps, pulling at his
bold moustache, anxiously jangling his keys

Some said she died with conscience clear as water: she flowed
from stream to stream to river's end; her songs were
scattered 'cross the seven seas

Some said she was cornered without knowing it: decidedly alive,
unmarred, coy, defenceless and alone

Some said she died with wilful diligence, carefully placing every
seed before she fell: the roses wound their roots about
her bones

Some said her path was paved with innocence: withered and de-
cried, even the starting pistol wept to see its job well
done

Some said it was her blood betrayed her: suddenly waking in the
    daylight, alarmed, boiling into silence, ever wary of the
    sun

She rose up from nowhere, gnashing her teeth, debased, wrecked,
    until the rain washed her fragments into cracks be-
    tween the rocks

Wracked with restless admonition, her final breath took flight
    upon the wind, whispering a lover's name, a secret
    kept, a lie foretold . . . Miraculous!

A Personal Extroduction from Text Number Ten

By ████████

Whilst thumbing my way through a vast pile of often tawdry and overlong pieces I was initially surprised to come across this piece, not so much due to its quality, but due to its form and content; for in many ways it fails in fitting any of the prerequisites of a true or even a quasi-*palmeresque*. Were it not for the title there would be no indication that it referred to Amanda at all! Nonetheless, it was immediately refreshing, particularly in the context of the other eight hundred or so pieces I was having to consider, and the more I reread it the more I was taken by its vibrant images, rich flavours and uplifting spirit.

Formally it falls into three "verses", each with a notional chorus line, concluding with the word *miraculous*. Each "verse" consists of six sentences or statements, each one fairly long, written essentially as prose without regularity of rhythm, and grouped in three rhyming couplets. But overall it strikes me as more of an invocation than a poem, conjuring the creation, turn of fate and ultimate destruction of a magical muse-like creature. It is rich in omens and superstition, as if spoken by a shaman as part of some ancient pagan ritual, and yet it is also strangely innocent—something that might be read to a child. The first "verse" draws from nature and the elements for its imagery, implying her spontaneous creation as some form of nature goddess, the spirit of Art; the second "verse" sees the corrupting influence of worldly concerns, clothes, money, dice, which draws to the fore the beast within—it is this that turns her fortune towards destruction; the third and final "verse" presents her death as a willing dissipation back into the fundamental elements from which she came, *not with a bang but a whimper*. In this narrative it is a fair depiction of the shining light that was Amanda Palmer in her brief flight through our world.

In the end I chose this piece because I found it to be positive and uplifting in its presentation of Amanda's life and death, which certainly made it stand out amongst the many more self-indulgent, self-pitying, violent, shocking, and downright depressing examples I had to plough through having foolishly agreed to be a part of this editorial board.

ON THE MANY CRIMES OF TOBIAS JAMES

This picture, taken at Luigi's Victorian Photographic Emporium, Soho, New York, in January 2008, is the only known image of "Tobias James", uncharacteristically on this occasion without a false moustache.

APPENDIX I

Editor's Introduction to the Appendices

As has already been stated in the *Preface to the Second Edition,* on 27th August 2007 all copies of the first edition were seized by the Boston Police Department, on the grounds that *Text Number Nine* bore an "extraordinary and incriminating resemblance" to the actual circumstances of Miss Palmer's death. There then followed a lengthy and thorough investigation into the relationship between the APT and the text in question, how and why it was chosen, where it was sourced etc. Naturally all at the APT felt at the time that there was no need for undue concern, however as the investigation progressed, it became rapidly apparent that the Editorial Board involved in the preparation of this book had, each in their own way, been touched by corruption, and manipulated into unprofessional behaviours not befitting a role of such high regard and responsibility. Indeed, piece by piece it became apparent that not one of the texts had, in reality, been chosen by the allocated editor, but instead had each been effectively planted by person or persons unknown, using methods including bribery, blackmail, social embarrassment, and in one case the inducing of paranoia. Ultimately all pending charges were dropped against the APT and those associated with it, however, despite the concluding resignations, many questions were left unanswered.

The APT Legal Department had, in the course of preparing a defence (given the possibility that charges may not have been dropped) acquired copies of much of the evidence gathered by the police, including all of the witness statements, lists of email and web addresses, dates, times, names, and many reports by internet researchers, forensic literary specialists, theoretical psychologists, etc, together with a single photograph, credited with being the only known image of Tobias James. After an extensive period of negotiation involving suits and counter-suits on either side it was finally agreed that we would be permitted to publish an account of our understanding of what had occurred, including whatever evidence we had at our disposal, under the unambiguous stricture that no information deemed to be of a sensitive or incriminating nature be published, with specific regard to the ongoing investigation into the death of Miss Palmer and any link that may or may not lead to Mr. James. It is worth the reader noting that the Boston Police Department (BPD) has successfully demanded final editorial control and under ███████████████   ████████ ███████ was ultimately granted full rights to ████████████ ███████████████████████████ wherever they deem appropriate.

APPENDIX II

The Case Against "Tobias James"

Following the seizure of *Text Number Nine*, and an initial inter-rogation of the Editorial Board, the BPD Internet Crime Unit (ICU) turned its attention towards tracking the author through cyber-space. The APT had, in the course of researching the *palmeresque* project, kept detailed records of every website a given text appeared on, and the earliest posting date, so far as we could tell, and so these, and any other related records, were all willingly handed over to Inspector Ruecker, together with our commitment to absolute cooperation.

Internet crime investigation is a slow and tedious process. By all accounts it takes place in a small office cubicle, and involves lit-tle more than copying and pasting text into search engines and oc-casionally sending emails to website administrators in the hope that a lead might be stumbled upon. For four months the APT re-mained in hiatus, publicly discredited, with charges pending against a number of senior board members, but nothing was hap-pening. Until we were either exonerated or formally charged we were legally bound not to publish a denial or defence against the many exaggerated rumours that were appearing in blogs and oc-casional newspaper articles. Our hard won reputation as an Arts funding body and arbiter of taste was clearly suffering. Finally our computers were returned and we could at least continue with running our business, but it seemed that this cloud of suspicion had made many of our former associates and contacts a little nervous, and they were no longer answering emails or phone calls, hence, in January 2008 the APT Legal Department began planning its extensive suit for compensation against the BPD.

That was until the second round of revelations.

As part of their investigation the BPD had hired a small team of forensic literary analysts led by a Dr. Ruth Weitz. Their job was to produce, through detailed analysis of the text, a psychological profile and notional biography of the author. Upon receipt of Dr. Weitz's report Inspector Ruecker immediately ordered the arrest of the entire Editorial Board once again, this time on charges of Literary Fraud and obstructing the police. Naturally the majority of the report remains under legal orders, however, the specific passages that led to these arrests are neither concerned with the psychology of the author, nor the circumstances of death of Amanda Palmer, and are therefore un-restricted:

> . . . *Given then that we had therefore established certain stylistic and formalistic similarities between all ten texts present in the book, we then set about demonstrating this postulation beyond all reasonable doubt. To do so we first isolated what we considered to be the main characteristics of concern within the texts (Christian religious symbolism,* ▮▮▮▮▮▮▮*, representations of restrained or repressed violence, formalised use of English sentence structuring,* ▮▮▮▮▮▮*, psychological obsession with the subject, misuse of colloquialisms,* ▮▮▮▮▮▮*, and* ▮▮▮▮▮▮*) and then, utilising the Gilmore System, we devised a series of scales with which to measure and score each text on that characteristic. We then plotted these scores on simple line graphs. When superimposed upon each other it becomes clear that each text demonstrates a remarkably similar series of ratios between each of the chosen characteristics...*

> . . . ▮▮▮▮▮▮▮▮▮▮▮▮▮▮▮▮▮▮▮▮▮▮▮▮▮

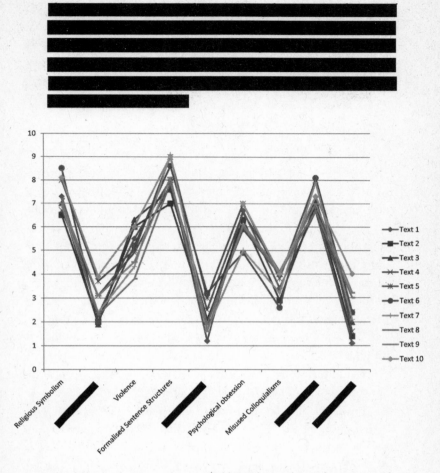

The above graph presents the remarkable similarity of ratios between specific relevant characteristics across all ten texts, thus demonstrating the single author postulation. The probability of a random series of ten texts showing equivalent similarities has been calculated at 1:3628800

. . . it is therefore, in my opinion and in the opinion of my colleagues, clear beyond any doubt whatever that each of the ten texts were written by the same author, with only the most superficial of efforts having been made to disguise their dis-

tinctive style including sentence structure, punctuation and habitual themes. Furthermore, taken as a whole this collection of stories, poems and essays reveal ███████████
████████████████████████████████████
████████████████████████████████████
████████████████████████████████████

Despite our initial incredulity at such an extraordinary claim, thirty-two hours of interrogation later a full set of confessions had been extracted, and they certainly made for astonishing reading, at least amongst the Legal Department of APT. It seemed that every member of the Editorial Board had been "nobbled" in some way or other. A number of cases were very similar: said editor was approached and befriended by a tall slim and handsome young man whilst at a bar, in a restaurant, shopping for stationary and in one case at a swimming pool. He was, by all accounts, effortlessly charming, well-dressed and in each case went under a different name. It is possibly worth mentioning that on every occasion the young gentleman was wearing a false moustache, although the style was clearly different for each editor (this may at first seem unusual, however it must be remembered that since the huge critical success of the video for *Where Did I Put My Shoes?* in February 2004, false moustaches have been very much in vogue amongst Miss Palmer's fans, often of both sexes). It has been agreed between members of the previous, now disgraced, Editorial Board and the present Directors of APT that in exchange for frank and honest accounts of what exactly had transpired no explicit details would be published, including any names. Regrettably it is therefore impossible at this stage to present any specifics with regard to how the mysterious gentleman achieved this extraordinary feat of manipulation. Very much in general it could be said that having first inveigled his way into one of various potential positions of trust, he then sought out a weakness, or insecurity of some kind that he would be able to involve himself with, thus enabling gentle pressure to reap rewards.

In each case the editor in question was, it seems, completely un-aware that this man was the author of the chosen text (each swears with much adamancy that the chosen text was amongst their given selection previous to his involvement—a claim later verified through meticulous cross-referencing). He had then somehow persuaded them to allow him to make the final choice (and to write the extroduction). They each claimed to feel, at the time, that it was merely a harmless delegation of responsibility, and had no idea that this same gentleman was involved in any way with other editors on the *palmeresque* project.

Thus, all amongst us who retained an interest in protecting the honour of the APT were left with a number of important questions, as the following minutes from the first meeting the new Directorial Committee of the APT on 17th March 2008 demonstrate:

Questions to be investigated and discussed at next meeting:

- *Who was this young man?*

- *Were the similarities of style between the chosen texts merely due to all the texts having been selected by this single man, no doubt with his own agenda? And if so could it be that he was drawn to particular themes and sentence structures intuitively or directly, and was not, therefore, a sole author.*

- *Were all the encounters with the same young man, or were there coincidentally a number of falsely-moustachioed young male Amanda Palmer fans attempting independ-ently to influence the selections for the book?' an unlikely but nonetheless possible scenario, needs to be considered.*

- *Was this man the author himself or did he work for another? (If working for another then more credence can be given to the multiple young men theory as the false moustaches could merely be a ruse to make us assume that it was all the same man).*

- *What could be the possible motive behind going to that much trouble to influence the choices of example texts in a small book about fan literature for a dead popstar?*

A few weeks after that meeting the BPD ICU had their first major break. They had been tracking a blog site user known to have put up a version of *Text Number Nine* through a series of bogus email addresses and server relays and had finally traced the source to recent activity from an IP address at an internet cafe in El Cerrito, across the bay from San Francisco. A Digital Technology virtual stake-out was put in place and within three days was duly rewarded when the computer in booth number three logged into one of a number of associated web accounts. The local police department was immediately notified and a team of detectives were mobilised to intercept the suspect. It had clearly been assumed that once logged into his account the suspect would spend a considerable amount of time online as the officers didn't arrive for a further fifty minutes by which time the suspect had already fled. Bob Parkes, manager of the internet cafe stated in an interview with an APT researcher:

> *... The young man suddenly appeared startled by something he had seen onscreen, frantically pressed at a few keys, then grabbed his coat and skedaddled. He was in such a hurry he left a memory card in the card reader, and when his wallet fell from his coat pocket he didn't even turn back to get it ... [The wallet contained] around eighty bucks, an antique photograph and a library card in the name of Tobias James ... About ten minutes later the cops arrived ...*

The library card turned out to be for membership of a small local library in Colindale, North-West London, England; it is currently unknown whether Tobias James is a real or assumed name. The photograph was recently taken by a novelty photographic studio in SoHo, New York, that specialises in the recreation of Victorian style photo-portraits, complete with digital fading and stains. It was later confirmed by all who are known to have met him, that the image in the photograph was indeed that of the man who had manipulated his way into editorial control of the first edition of this book, albeit without his characteristic false moustache. Most compelling of all was the memory card, which contained a remarkable one-hundred-and-ninety-seven *palmeresques*, many incomplete, some fragmentary, and amongst them, all ten texts chosen for the first edition. In every case where the text was found to have been already uploaded to the internet the creation date on the memory card pre-dated the earliest known posting, making it almost certain that these were original works by a single author. However, this new evidence must have provided the BPD with new leads as shortly after the failed apprehension of Mr James all charges against the APT were dropped, and as a result, the APT Legal Department was no longer in a position to apply for copies of any new evidence that may be used against them. Hence we have no further knowledge of the ongoing police investigation into either Tobias James, or the death of Amanda Palmer. What we can be sure of is that the man who we have come to know as Tobias James did indeed, beyond any reasonable doubt, write all of the texts selected for this volume, and, for reasons unknown, went to very great effort to ensure editorial control over their selection. Any involvement he may have had in the death of Miss Palmer remains a police matter, and though we at the APT have our suspicions, they are best, at present, kept to ourselves.

However, we are not alone in any suspicion we may have of the man known as Tobias James: in a recent edition of *Rue-Morgue Magazine* readers voted James number four in their top ten suspects for involvement in the killing of Miss Palmer. Although we at the APT would be the first to acknowledge that a popularity contest is rarely the best forum for judging character this does at least demonstrate that his great literary fraud has somewhat caught the public imagination, and, as they say, "not necessarily in a good way".

APPENDIX III

Who Is Tobias James?—a brief biography

Regrettably this appendix must be all too brief and none too biographical, as little, if anything beyond the evidence already mentioned, is actually known about Mr. James. However, by applying a detective's eye to that which we do have, a certain amount can be deduced.

Firstly, then, the hearsay evidence - from statements made by the various editors he encountered we know:

- He is in his early-to-mid twenties, well educated, softly spoken with a slight Alabama accent and the occasional hint of English affectation. He is clearly very capable of keeping up an intelligent conversation on a wide variety of subjects, from Science and the Arts to pop culture and politics, always generously topped off with a compelling and occasionally frustrating sprinkling of trivia.

- He spoke at length to a number of editors about his travels around Europe, particular time spent in England, Norway and Albania, and was apparently very convincing in this, suggesting that such a trip may well have been taken.

- He was very careful not to answer any questions about

(or make any reference to) his family, and was, by all accounts, a master of the subtle subject change.

- He often made the claim that he was a poet, albeit as yet unpublished.

The false moustaches he wore were always of the very highest quality, made from real human facial hair and virtually indistinguishable from the real thing. One editor states that Mr. James had mentioned that his moustaches were made to measure by *Proctor & Gladwin*, of London's Saville Row. They have refused to "pass comment on any specific individual customer account". They did, however, acknowledge that they have "in the past, and upon occasion, supplied bespoke moustaches to certain clients".

Then we have the evidence of the wallet and its contents. Let's start with the wallet itself. It is a finely stitched eel-skin wallet, designed to be kept thin and free from any excess of documents or notes; a very tidy and organised man's wallet. There is no place to keep coins. Inside it is modestly stamped E. Goodrich & sons, a Cambridge maker of gentleman's leather-ware. The wallet's most notable feature is however on the outside, which is embossed with an elaborate gold-chased monogram. The APT faxed a tracing of the monogram design to E. Goodrich & sons enquiring if they had any records of who it may have been made for and received the following reply:

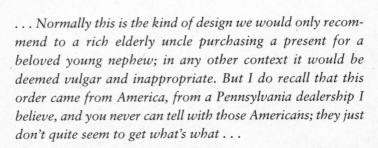

. . . Normally this is the kind of design we would only recommend to a rich elderly uncle purchasing a present for a beloved young nephew; in any other context it would be deemed vulgar and inappropriate. But I do recall that this order came from America, from a Pennsylvania dealership I believe, and you never can tell with those Americans; they just don't quite seem to get what's what . . .

It is also interesting that the monogram puts the J before the T which could indicate a name of James Tobias, however we have since learnt that had the wallet indeed been purchased by a rich elderly uncle for a beloved young nephew it would not be at all uncommon for the initial of the surname to be placed first, as English etiquette, and therefore sadly American pretention, traditionally demands.

Now let us consider the library card. It is a standard membership card for a small local library in Colindale, Borough of Barnet, North West London. To become a member all Barnet libraries require two utility bills in the members name as address verification, and further research has revealed that a Tobias James held accounts with both EDF Energy and British Gas from February 16th, 2006 to August 21st, 2006, registered at Flat B, 5 Ableton Drive, Hendon. We have also learnt that Barnet council employees are much more open to flattery and persuasion than English gentleman's tailors, as we were able to easily acquire a full list of the books borrowed by Mr. James:

- *The Little Book of Sayings of Oscar Wilde* edited by Alexander Noble.

- *Who's Who in British History, Late Hanoverian Britain,* 1789-1837.

- *A Macabre Miscellany* by Geoffrey Abbott.

- *The Vulgar Tongue, Buckish Slang and Pickpocket Eloquence* by Francis Grose.

- *The City of Dreadful Night* by James Thomson.

- *Origins of the Popular Style, The Antecedents of Twentieth Century Popular Music* by Peter Van Der Merwe.

- *An Incomplete History of the Art of Funerary Violin* by Rohan Kriwaczek.

- *Nazi Literature in the Americas* by Roberto Bolano.

- *British Mousetraps and their Makers* by David Drummond.

- *My Secret Life, The Sex Diaries of a Victorian Gentleman, Volume One, Early Memories* by "Walter".

On receiving this list it was immediately clear to us that we had the right Tobias James in our sights, as it effectively verified much of the previously known hearsay evidence. Clearly he had spent some time in Europe; the confirmation that the card was genuine proved that. His reported knowledgeable eloquence and delight in trivia were, it seems, a much-studied art, judging by the predominance of reference materials and books on vocabulary and quotable comment. There were also a fair proportion of books concerned with the later nineteenth century, and, as will be discussed in the following chapter, the writing of Tobias James exhibits a strong concern with the elegance of late nineteenth-century register and formality. The inclusion of my own book on the history of Funerary Violin strongly implies that he was at the time researching the Directorial Board of the APT, and may have already been aware of the *palmeresque* project. In addition we also learnt from Colindale Library that *My Secret Life* was never returned, and as a result Mr. James currently owes £31.86 in overdue fines (on the day of writing).

And then there is, of course, the most compelling piece of evidence: the photograph. It was taken at Luigi's Victorian Photographic Emporium, SoHo, New York, on January 17th 2008—the address and logo are clearly printed on the back card, in the manner of nineteenth-century photographs. Luigi's, as their full name suggests, specialises in reproducing the look of Victorian photographs through the use of original period equipment. They also have available a full stock of period costumes and props.

The first thing(s) to jump out at you are the eyes: they are very intense and you can almost see the whites all the way around the pupils; they seem to bulge outwards just a little. All this suggests that the subject might be suffering from a thyroid condition. If that is the case he may well be exhibiting one or more of a number of possible symptoms: fatigue; depression/anxiety/paranoia; muscle aches and pains; bowel problems; and swelling of the neck and eyes. This would also account for the time he has clearly had available for the thorough digestion of reading materials, a common form of escapism amongst habitually ill persons.

The next thing to note is the clothing. Luigi, who turned out to be a very affable and helpful fellow despite the persona he likes to project, recalled that Mr. James had not hired a costume as he had arrived ready attired. Luigi particularly noticed at the time that Mr. James had been wearing a splendidly twirled Victorian-style moustache which Luigi had assumed to be real, and indeed admired, but Mr. James had then removed it for the photo-shoot, carefully placing it in a small silver moustache-shaped box. After the shoot, the moustache was reattached before Mr. James left with his developed and printed picture. All of the above strongly suggests a man rich in affectation and with something of a fetish for Victoriana, both traits that are further demonstrated in his writing, as will be discussed in the following chapter.

Finally we come to the memory card. It is regrettable that the BPD has found it necessary to withhold the contents of this memory card as there is little doubt that it must contain many items of specific and general interest to all scholars of the *palmeresque*. We do know that it holds one hundred and ninety-seven texts, a number of them incomplete, and includes amongst them the ten texts from the first edition of this book. It is further thought, though as yet unconfirmed, that some amongst those ten texts appear on the memory card in an amended or developed form, suggesting that Mr. James is a *tinkerer;* a man who finds it hard to consider his works finished and let them go—these amendments were clearly made for his own benefit alone, as there was no possibility of publication for the developed versions. We have also discovered that the username Tobias_James has been banned from editing articles on Wikipedia together with twelve other associated email accounts that were linked to a traced IP address. The reason given is "fictionalisation and falsification, although we commend him on his wit".

And therefore, to summarise; if a brief biography of Tobias James were to be postulated it would quite possibly read something along the following lines:

Tobias James was most likely born to a wealthy and long-established family that valued education, possibly in Alabama, later perhaps moving to New York when he was around eight. He may have a wealthy uncle who lives in Pennsylvania. He was probably a sickly child and teenager but doubtless worked hard at school, later possibly winning himself a place at Columbia University, or perhaps Cambridge University, England, though in all likelihood under a different name. After graduating he is thought to have travelled around Europe, possibly spending an unknown amount of time in Norway and Albania before arriving in England some time before February 16th 2006, where he based himself in Hendon, North West London. He probably returned to America some time after 21st August 2006. He may or may not be in possession of a private income. At some point, most likely after May 13th 2002 he began writing texts referring to or inspired by the death of Amanda Palmer. He has by now nearly completed at least one hundred and ninety-seven. During the period from October 2006 to July 2007 he systematically manipulated his way into a position of editorial control over the book *On the Many Deaths of Amanda Palmer*. He is currently one of eleven people on the BPD's prime suspect list for the murder of Amanda Palmer. His current whereabouts are unknown, however ███████████████████████████████████████
███████████████████████████████████████
███████████████████████████████████████
███████████████████████████████████████

He also enjoys uploading spurious and made-up articles to Wikipedia, many of which relate to a circle of invented nineteenth-century poets known as the Devonshire Cathartists.

Of course, much of the above is, by necessity, mere speculation.

APPENDIX IV

On the Writing of Tobias James—
a Psychological Analysis

Having been impressed by how much had been revealed in Dr. Weitz's admirable report on the writing of Tobias James for the BPD we at the APT decided to commission our own literary forensic specialist, on this occasion a Dr. E. Simmons, and her team. The report she produced was nothing if not thorough, amounting to nearly four hundred pages and hence will not be printed in full here. Instead we will present selected passages from the chapter summaries and introductions.

Simmons opens her report with an explanation of her division of perspectives:

> *. . . It is therefore impossible to draw any valuable conclusions with regard to the psychological makeup of this individual without considering the question of* Text Number Nine. *If, as the BPD suggests, the text does indeed bear a "remarkable and incriminating resemblance" to the scene of Palmer's death, this detail has to be factored into our analysis. It seems that there are three possible explanations:*

> *1. That it is mere coincidence. It seems that James has written at least 197 such texts and it is therefore not impossible that*

his imagination had stumbled unknowingly upon the right set of ingredients. In this case the entire project would have to be considered an innocent expression of an Obsessive Compulsive Disorder.

2. *That, at some point, either before or after he started writing these texts, James had met the murderer and been told the details of the crime. This could have occurred either in the real or the virtual world. If this is the case, it could be that James' writing caused the perpetrator to approach him, or that the meeting itself triggered his writing, a shock which would therefore provide justifiable cause for his future obsessive writing behaviour as a form of catharsis.*

3. *That James was either the murderer himself, or was involved first hand with the murder, hence the details of the crime would be well known to him, and his obsessive writing on the subject could be driven by the purging of guilt and disguising of the crime.*

   I will therefore at times, where relevant, divide my analyses into three categories which will henceforth be referred to as Perspective 1, Perspective 2 and Perspective 3.

She then goes on to consider the various qualities of the writing in general:

. . . Throughout James displays a technical mastery of the mechanics of the English language, utilising a great variety of sentence structures, tenses, time-scales, perspectives etc; however, underlying each text are a number of consistent qualities that make any pretence at multiple authorship merely notional:

1. *James is clearly drawn towards formalised "correct" English, even when the context of the writing might be better served by something more colloquial. He also, given any ap-*

propriate (or not so) opportunity, will habitually slip into a more old-fashioned higher registered tone, particularly when versifying. These traits appear in every text available for examination.

2. James has a tendency to moralise, a trait that is increasingly rare amongst today's writers. Every text reads like it is trying to make a point, impart a moral lesson, or reveal some kind of "truth" (as he sees it).

3. The whole collection is shot through with religious and/or spiritual symbolism. Miss Palmer is variously cast as a disembodied soul on a spiritual journey (texts numbered 2, 4, 7); an incarnation of the Devil (text 3); Jesus on the cross (text 8); a Madonna-like figure whose death is transfigured into a spirit child born of song (text 5); a flawed manifestation of the Godhead itself (text 9); a magical spirit creature (text 10): the only two exceptions are text 1, in which she is the innocent victim of magic, and text 6, the driest of all the texts, in which she dies attempting to restore spiritual import to a debased ritual.

4. A number of the stories centre around a specific moment of culmination with lines such as "she had made it, all the way to the very top" (text 1) and "you will remain forever at your peak, the pinnacle, your very greatest of moments" (text 4). In other texts these central moments are more subtly placed but are nonetheless strongly present.

5. There is a distinct undercurrent of ████████████ ███████████████████████████████████████ █████████████████████████████ often to great comical effect, albeit at times misjudged and in bad taste.

6. Although expressed differently in each case, it is clear that every text has been written within the confines of a specific set of rules, as if the author is playing a game of literary technique: "in this text I will only use dialogue only once at the

focal point" (text 1); "in this text I will alternate between showing and telling the story with each paragraph" (text 7); "in this text I limit myself to formalised turn of the 20th century language" (text 2) etc... This suggests he may be offering a nod to the notion of multiple authorships, though he makes little effort to fulfil it through any other means.

The report then launches into a detailed discussion on some of the more revealing psychological qualities of the individual texts. The following passages are taken from the summary paragraphs:

> *. . . It has therefore been demonstrated that the themes presented amongst the texts in this collection can be broadly placed in three categories:*
>
> *1. Miss Palmer as a victim of magical/spiritual forces beyond her control (texts 1, 4, 7, 9)*
>
> *2. Miss Palmer's death as a form of transfiguration (texts 2, 3, 5, 8, 9, 10).*
>
> *3. Miss Palmer brings her death upon herself (texts 2, 6, 7, 9).*

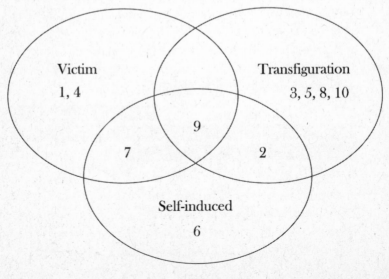

216

. . . It is also worth noting, despite being somewhat obvious, the format of the texts: texts 1, 2, 4, 7 and 8 are all written as fictional prose; texts 3, 5 and 10 are written in rhyming verse; text 6 is written in essay form; and text 9 effortlessly veers between prose, verse and essays forms.

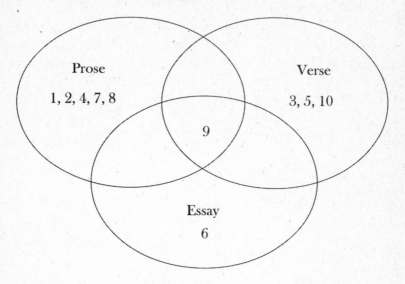

. . . It is however in his portrayals of himself as the "man with the false moustache" that James is at his most psychologically revealing. This character, in one form or another, appears in every text; although in some texts the falseness of the moustache itself is not specifically mentioned, it is however reasonable to assume, amongst this particular collection, that characters such as Silas Monger (text 1), Jamie and Filch (text 7) and Father Stringer (text 8) are in fact wearing false moustaches, but that they are well fitted bespoke moustaches and thus easily mistaken for the real thing, as has been previously demonstrated. As the moustachioed gentleman James variously portrays himself as a guide who leads Miss Palmer into a new magical world (texts 2, 4, 7, 9); a manipulative and controlling force

against which Miss Palmer seems helpless (texts 1, 7, 9); and a character for whom Miss Palmer's death unleashes a consummate act of creativity on their part (text 5, 8, 9). In text 6 and 9 he places himself as an essential non-participatory link in the corrupting of the tradition that ultimately leads to Miss Palmer's death; in texts 9 and 10 he places himself as the all-knowing narrator who prophesies Miss Palmer's magical existence, turn of Fate and ultimate dissipation. It is also worth noting that rarely in any of the texts are two falsely-moustachioed men present at one time, and when they are (text 7) one seeks to destroy the other. This further indicates James' use of the writing process to work through his own inner conflicts in a quite literal literary manner.

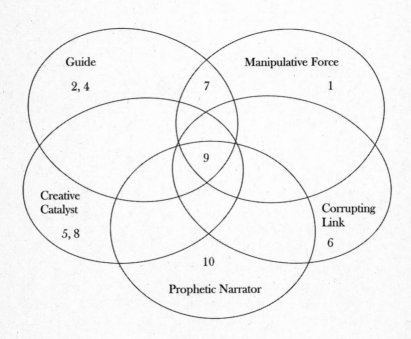

. . . What becomes apparent when these and other sets of simple observation are plotted in the form of Venn diagrams is that text 9 invariably falls at the very centre. In total we plotted 27 different sets of criteria and in only 2 diagrams was text 9 outside the central zone of inclusivity: one involving the frequency with which the words ████, ███████, ██████ *and* ███ *were used, the other focussing specifically on Miss Palmer's* █████████████████████████ ██████ *. . .*

The report then goes into much detail with regard to the various possible implications of this observation which regrettably cannot be printed here due to the many quotations it includes from Text Number Nine, without which it would make little sense. It does, however offer the following generalised (and therefore less "sensitive") conclusion:

. . . It is therefore clear that text 9 is in every sense the emotional, thematic, psychological, and technical centre of the collection. . . . Indeed it contains within its lines every literary technique and theme employed in the other texts put together, only in a far more condensed and deliberate form . . .

. . . The overriding impression is that this text 9 was probably the first text to be written, most likely in a fit of excited creative angst, and that the other 9 texts (and in all likelihood the further 187 texts which have been withheld from our examination) were an attempt to unravel the density of text 9 and recapture something of the artistic excitement that accompanied its creation . . .

In addition to these specific observations the report also summarises a number of other themes running through the texts:

. . . Given the nature of Miss Palmer's work, which is undeniably shot through with gratuitous sexuality, we must take a

moment to consider the sexual content of the texts, which is all the more present through its absence. Despite the moustachioed gentleman having Miss Palmer in his power in a number of the stories, at no point is there any hint of sexual attraction or motivation. It is however most revealing that in text 8, once Father Stringer (the moustachioed gentleman) has left the scene, there is more than a hint of sexual attraction from young Mary-Beth towards Miss Palmer. This passage is beautifully and subtly written clearly demonstrating James' awareness of, and appreciation for, Miss Palmer's much flaunted sexual allure. That he places the onus of demonstration upon a young girl, and therefore not upon a representation of himself suggests a certain disassociation within his own sexuality. This is then further demonstrated in text 9, in which ██

██
██
██
██
██
██

although admittedly this is all cleverly implied without ever being explicitly stated. Put together these two texts suggest a man who is ill at ease with his own sexual attraction towards Miss Palmer, possibly as a result of actions he had undertaken in the past (Perspective Three) or frustration at inaction when faced with opportunities for gratification unfulfilled (Perspective Two) . . .

. . . As with sexuality, there is a similar dissociation with violence against Miss Palmer. Although in the majority of texts Miss Palmer's death is either not portrayed or comes about in a non-violent manner, it is once again the few exceptions that are most revealing. In text 5 the moustachioed gentleman (representing James) comes upon the dying Miss Palmer, who has been stabbed for no valuable reason, and through this encounter discovers the inspiration to write a great work, thus giving her death meaning. This is a theme further developed in text 9, by far the most violent of all the texts, albeit in a subtly implied manner. Here we see 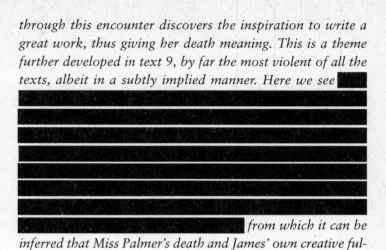 from which it can be inferred that Miss Palmer's death and James' own creative fulfilment are inextricably linked, and that the degree of violence levelled against Miss Palmer is presented as directly proportional to James' own artistic achievement . ..

. . . Having looked closely at all the texts and the themes within we can therefore draw the following conclusions with regard to the three possible perspectives:

Perspective One (coincidental origination): as we have seen, the centrality of text 9 renders this perspective exceptionally unlikely at best. This perspective can therefore be largely dismissed.

Perspective Two (origination in reaction to shock): this perspective appears to fit the available evidence best, the most likely implied scenario being as follows—James stumbles inadvertently upon the scene of Miss Palmer's demise—he watches from the distance, shocked at both what he is seeing and his own reaction to the sight; in addition finding it uncomfortably sexually exciting—in a state of near hysteria he returns home and, being of a sensitive artistic bent, launches into an inspired fit of writing resulting in text 9—following this he is haunted by the ecstatic thrill of cathartic creation and begins obsessively attempting to reach that peak once again by recasting the characters and scenes, but to no avail

—eventually he comes to believe that publication is his only chance for resolution, and so, having heard about the book being researched for the Amanda Palmer Trust, embarks upon a series of highly sophisticated schemes, many involving criminal forms of manipulation, to essentially highjack editorial control of the selection process, naturally choosing exclusively his own works.

Perspective Three (origination as an attempt to cleanse guilt at direct involvement): initially this perspective was considered a fair candidate, however, after further consideration it has been concluded that Perspective Three is not compatible with the number of, and variation of tone amongst, the presented texts. Had this writing been related directly to guilt many precedents suggest it would be more focussed around the actual events and less around fantastical and religious reinterpretations. In addition this perspective makes little sense of the quest towards control clearly expressed in a number of the texts. . . . had James been previously associated with Miss Palmer this perspective would fit the psychological profile better, however no evidence exists to suggest any previous contact. . . .

. . . We therefore feel fairly confident in offering the following psychological profile of Mr. Tobias James, with the cautionary reminder that, despite the wealth of evidence and well-established theory to hand; it is, in reality, little more than informed speculation:

Tobias James most likely suffers from an acute-displaced-Samson-complex-by-proxy, that being a deep-seated character-ological defect stemming from faulty object relations normally leading to existential despair and suicidal longing. In the case of Mr. James this complex is further complicated by a further addiction to control which prevents actual expression through any means other than representations, usually fictional, although at times spilling through into fictionalised physical presentations of himself. The resulting acute displace-

222

ment of the compulsion to re-enact a sudden unexpected in-
stant of betrayal and/or rage (most probably involving his
stumbling accidentally upon the scene of Miss Palmer's de-
mise) is thus expressed through the extensive and considerable
rewriting of events until they have become almost sanitised
by the act of repetition and the subsequent decay of intensity:
thus we would assume that those texts embodying acts of vi-
olence were among the first to be written, and those texts
which read more like children's parables would have been
written later . . . (It is worth noting that almost all the texts
portray betrayal in one sense or another) . . . This displace-
ment of the power to act into fictionalised territory is further
symbolised by his wearing a false moustache whilst presenting
himself to the world—and his removal of said moustache
when presenting his physical image to himself (such as in the
photographic studio) . . .

. . . We would therefore consider Mr. James to be highly
intelligent, manipulative, without scruples, a consummate liar,
and indeed a borderline sociopath, (all characteristics essential
in a writer of any real substance) although we would not con-
sider him to be dangerous in an immediate sense of the word.

It should be noted that all of the above are the opinions of Dr.
Simmons and her team, and do not necessarily reflect the opinions
of the editor, nor the Amanda Palmer Trust as a whole. They are
printed here for reference purposes only.

APPENDIX V

A Brief Comment on the Many Rumours and Speculations Surrounding Tobias James and the Death of Amanda Palmer

It is of course no great surprise that where facts fail to deliver, rumours flock to fill the gap, particularly in this age where speed of communication is measured in megabytes per second, publication on the internet remains entirely unregulated, and many millions of people spend their working days sat, bored, in front of networked computers. Quite how, and by whom, word of Tobias James (and the multiple frauds he committed against the APT) was first leaked remains unknown, despite our many efforts, but whatever few facts had been leaked were soon overshadowed by the many rumours and speculations that have, over recent months, been filling the pages of various chat-rooms and blog-sites. As has been clearly demonstrated we at the APT do indeed harbour many suspicions against Mr. James and most certainly feel he has a case to answer, however we would strongly caution the reader against taking too seriously any speculations which go beyond that which has already been presented here.

As is usually the case with rumours, they can be divided into four broad categories: those which are palpably absurd but somehow touch upon a desire in people for them to be true; those which are more plausible and yet have no basis whatever in fact; those that touch upon truth yet bend it considerably out of shape; and those that turn out to have been correct all along. In the interests of maintaining good relations with the BPD we have agreed to not mention any of those more plausible rumours lest we inadvertently reveal information currently deemed "sensitive", and instead present here a few of the more absurd and clearly unsubstantiated speculations currently making the rounds. As might be expected they include all the usual suspects:

- Alien abduction – that Mr. James was some form of shape-shifting alien shot down by the US Air Force over New Mexico, hence his lack of a recorded past; that his false moustache is worn to disguise his inability to mimic the human philtrum; that his mission is to capture a prime specimen of fertile breeding stock for medical experimentation back on his planet (it has been proposed by some that this particularly species may procreate through the exchange of vocalised sound frequencies, therefore effectively through song rather than physical contact, hence the choice of Miss Palmer). However, given Mr. James' clear command of written English/American idioms this seems unlikely. In addition, the one photograph we have of James clearly displays a fine example of a human philtrum.

- Government conspiracy – that Mr. James was an orphan who was adopted by an elite group within the CIA and trained from childhood for this particular type of infiltration mission. When the order came through that Miss Palmer was to be "taken out" he turned rogue and has placed her in a safe house having left a carefully constructed false trail. The texts he then placed in this book contain coded messages to other rogue cells and were they to be decoded they could bring down the whole CIA, if

226

not the US government. Again there is an obvious *however*... James is known to have left behind his memory card when fleeing the internet cafe, which is hardly what one would expect from a crack agent trained since childhood. In addition, there is no obvious reason why Miss Palmer would be considered any kind of threat to the US government.

- "Love child" – that Mr. James is Miss Palmer's son from a teenage affair attributed to many improbable men, and a few that, though more possible, are equally unlikely. Among the more extraordinary claims is that he is Miss Palmer's "love child" with John Denver, and it seems that in 1986, when in her early teens, Miss Palmer did indeed run away with the John Denver road-show for a week, however there is no evidence that she at any point became pregnant, nor gave birth to a child. In addition this rumour bears no relation to anything that we do know about Mr. James, nor does it attempt to explain his writing of the texts or the case of Text Number Nine. It is however interesting to note that though this rumour is entirely compatible with the government conspiracy rumour (had the love child been put up for adoption) no rumour we have come across has yet made this link.

- Love affair – that Mr. James and Miss Palmer had been conducting a secret love affair over the year previous to her apparent demise, and that the pressures of her extraordinary and sudden success as an artist and performer had pushed them both to the limit with regard to maintaining a healthy secret relationship. As a result Miss Palmer decided to stage her own death and Mr. James used all his many means to distract attention from this fact by sowing the seeds of discord and mistrust amongst all who knew her, and indeed all who are involved in investigating her death. This rumour might seem faintly plausible (though entirely unsubstantiated) were it not for the fact that Miss Palmer is well known to have had little or no interest in younger men, preferring considerably older men and, more often still, older women, for her sexual and love liaisons.

- Self perpetuation – that Mr. James himself is personally responsible for starting all of the above rumours and many others unmentioned in an attempt raise his own public profile and to generate intrigue and menace in the run-up to publication of this book, thus hoping to considerably boost sales and therefore his own royalty income and literary prestige. This rumour is among the more compelling, chiming as it does with an increased public understanding of the means and power of marketing ploys, however the APT can assure the reader that Mr. James will be receiving no royalties from sales of this book (all profits, if any, will go towards the funding of further APT artistic projects) nor does the APT have any contact whatsoever with Mr. James, or any idea as to his current whereabouts.

There are, of course, many further rumours and speculations, some of them more ludicrous, some more plausible, but all, as yet, entirely unsubstantiated. Those mentioned above are merely the most repeated. For the curious reader who wishes to take this line of research further a cursory internet search ("Amanda Palmer" "Tobias James") will reveal many thousands of pages that link the two names, in most cases directly, however, the APT wishes to make it clear that it in no way endorses the making of such a search, nor can it be held in any way responsible for the content of third party websites.

POSTSCRIPT

A Letter from Tobias James

Once again the run-up to publication of this second edition was interrupted in a most unexpected way. Around ten days prior to printing, just as the type-setting had been completed, the APT received a letter purporting to be from Tobias James himself. Immediately a meeting of the APT Board of Director's was called and, after surprisingly little debate it was unanimously agreed that the letter should be included, in full, as a postscript to this book, with the following cautionary comments:

1. It must be born in mind that there is no real evidence that this letter is from Tobias James himself, and that it could well be nothing more than a cynical hoax, possibly by one of the disgraced members of the previous Board of Directors who is known to bear a grudge against the APT for the public dishonour incurred due to the circumstances of his/her summary dismissal.
2. Even if understood to have been written by Mr. James there is no reason to assume that any of the statements or opinions contained within are in fact true or real as James has already demonstrated his consummate skills as a liar and manipulator many times over.

However, if the letter were proven at a later date to be genuine, and the statements and opinions it contains demonstrated to be true, it would seem inappropriate, nay irresponsible, for it not to be included here as it would effectively constitute major evidence in the case both for and against Mr. James.

Thus having fully emphasized all of the above points we offer the following text, in full, and with neither comment nor analysis, that you, the reader, might be in a position to make your own judgement:

Dear Mr. Kriwaczek, and indeed all at the APT who are involved in the palmeresque *project,*

I have read your little book with much interest and amusement—(please don't overly trouble yourselves with how: I can assure you there are no further issues with "corruption" or "nobbling" amongst your colleagues and associates, merely lax security on your internet server, something you might wish to address at a later date). And I must commend you on your wildly imaginative portrayal of the character "Tobias James"; alas, if only I were half as mysterious and enigmatic! And as for your psychological analysis—well, I need not remind you, I am sure, that all that stuff is merely made-up shit, invented by a pseudo-scientific industry whose only reason for existence is to make up more shit to justify its existence! Still, it made for an entertaining read, for me at least, but then who doesn't like reading about themselves, however absurd the contents.

But there is one important, nay, fundamental, point that you have missed, a point so essential that without grasping it you have largely misunderstood everything about my intentions and execution. Now don't get me wrong, I completely understand—it can indeed be hard to see beyond the petty bubbles in which we live and work—the human mind is after all a pattern seeking machine; it searches out meaning by recognising forms, rules, roles; then seeks reinforcement from others. That is what belief systems are; that is how societies are built; that is how cliques evolve: those little bubbles of self-importance founded upon shared understandings, however absurd or laughable. And thus I must imagine that all among you who work so diligently for the Amanda Palmer Trust, who each day enter that building, pass the paintings, the posters and that grotesque sculpture in the foyer, who then sit in your artsy offices devotedly promoting and developing the life, works and memory of Miss Amanda Palmer, must hold her in some awe indeed. To you she must by now have become an icon of sorts, almost a goddess, a martyr, a figurehead, a leader, the very glue that holds your organisation and its vision together. But you see, to me, and this is what your little book completely fails to grasp, to me Miss Palmer herself, alive or dead, is of no consequence whatsoever!

Certainly she was a popular singer, by all accounts fairly good at her job, but, frankly, so what! Sure, she wrote her own songs, and some, it is claimed, may even get close to being almost poetic, but again, so what! And yes, she "looked good in clothes", but so the fuck what! I mean, and I don't expect you to understand this, but does that shit really count for anything at all? I mean, really? On the scale of things? Did she cure cancer? Did she solve the global population crisis? Did she end, or even temper, famine in the third world? Did she make even the smallest difference to the many urgent and important issues facing humanity and human beings each and every day? No, no and again no! She was an entertainer, nothing more, nothing less. She got up on stage and pranced about in her underwear singing songs . . .

And yet, and yet . . . to her fans, and here I mean her real fans, those for whom her music has become a part their identity, to them she is, alive or dead, a magician with the power to transform, to comfort, to empower and inspire . . . or so it seems . . . and that is where my true fascination lies, not with Miss Palmer herself, but with the faith invested in her by her *fans, and the power they derive from it . . . Ok, re-reading that last passage I see I have allowed grandiloquence to cloud the issue, something of a habit of mine—what I mean to say is what really interests me, what made me involve myself with all this shit in the first place, is the imagined Miss Palmer, the Miss Palmer invented by the needs and requirements of her fans. The distinction is subtle and yet essential. It is <u>that</u> Miss Palmer whom I have been playing games with all along; it is <u>that</u> Miss Palmer whom I have killed repeatedly in hundreds of different ways, each born within the inevitable dichotomy between <u>that</u> Miss Palmer and her more "real" twin. The difference between the two is indeed both telling and painful. And now that the "real" Miss Palmer has been summarily dismissed from the equation, <u>that</u> Miss Palmer's power seems to be growing un-checked, for a while at least. Thus I felt it was my duty to meddle, to see if these things could be subverted, for the experiment, for the fun of it all. So please do not confuse the one issue with the other.*

As for the questions you are no doubt keen to have me answer: am I really the author of all the texts including Text Number Nine? Was I in some way involved with Miss Palmer's death? Did I witness it? Am I really a criminal mastermind who has turned all my powers towards infiltrating the editorial board of a small time Arts organisation for no profit other than self-satisfaction? . . .

Well, I wouldn't want to spoil all your fun just yet . . .

But I will say this, you were right about my wallet—it was indeed a gift from my "elderly" uncle.

Most sincerely, Tobias James.

About the Editor

ROWEN KAYE was born in 1961 to a Hungarian father and French Mother living in Cricklewood, North London. (He changed his name to Rohan Kriwaczek to "outwardly express [his] inner exoticism" in 1981.) Young Rowen was a problem child from the beginning, and spent a great deal of his

youth in and out of hospital for various, usually self-induced, injuries and illnesses. He left school at seventeen having achieved less than the bare minimum and spent the following fifteen years making little if any impression upon a remarkable number of artistic professions: illustrator, poet, composer, choreographer, interior designer, historical-hoaxer, plumber, musician, dramaturge, theoretical tap-dancer; it wasn't until he became involved with the Guild of Funerary Violinists in the mid 1990s that he finally found his vocation as a gifted artistic executor, quickly rising to the position of Acting President of the venerable Guild. Following his evident success in that post he took on the additional role of Executive Curator for the Rohan Theatre in 2000, (the similarity of name is merely a coincidence), later re-establishing the Rohan Theatre Band and developing a new younger fan-base for the once celebrated institution.

It was in the aftermath of the Rohan Theatre Band's now notorious "final gig", (a show which left emotional and in some cases physical scars on all who attended), that Kriwaczek first stumbled upon Amanda Palmer amidst the wreckage of the venue, suffering from a broken ankle and severe shock. That proved to be the beginning of a life-long friendship that was only ended by Miss Palmer's tragic death eighteen months later.

With the establishment of the Amanda Palmer Trust in 2006 Kriwaczek took on the role first of General Secretary and then later as Associate Chairman and Contributing Editor, before stepping down in 2009, although he is still actively involved in many APT funded projects.

Kriwaczek has, over the past ten years, been the recipient of numerous accolades and awards for his various contributions to the arts and funerary industries, although, with typical modesty, he has asked for them not to be listed here. He is, however, proud to mention his bronze medal in the "Most Luxurious Imperial" category of the International Beard and Moustache Tournament 2007.

An Incomplete History of the Art of Funerary Violin

It is only by staring Death in the face that you can truly say you have known Life; it is only by losing that which you hold most dear that you can truly say you have known Love; such is the Art of the Funerary Violinist.

From its origins in the Elizabethan Protestant Reformation, to its final extinction amidst the guns of the First World War, the art of Funerary Violin was characterized by many unique and frequently misunderstood qualities that set it apart from all other forms of music. Despite its enormous influence on classical music generally and on the Romantic Movement in particular, this music has almost entirely vanished. In a series of 'funerary purges', the art of funerary violin was condemned as 'the music of the devil' and the Guild of Funerary Violinists driven into silence or clandestine activity. This is the music that, despite all attempts at suppression, has haunted Europe's collective unconscious for more than a century. Now Rohan Kriwaczek reveals its incredible history. Painstakingly pieced together from a handful of fragments and unsubstantiated and frequently unspoken rumours, and making use of a number of extraordinary recent discoveries, *An Incomplete History of the Art of Funerary Violin* celebrates a unique musical tradition that refuses to die.

'The Art of the Funerary Violin is a fascinating work in its own right, an unorthodox alternative history novel filled with left-field characters and quirky details.' - Sydney Morning Herald

'This truly is a bizarre book' – The New Statesman

'In seinen besten momenten streift dieses scurrile und sehr britische Buch den Humor von Sternes „Tristrum Shandy" oder Boswells „Dr. Johnson".' - Frankfurter Allgemeine Zeitung

For more information on Funerary Violin, and to hear samples
of the music and purchase CDs please visit
www.guildoffuneraryviolinists.org.uk

Recordings by Rohan Kriwaczek

Solo Studio albums

Ghost Train

New Ritual Dark Music

Walking East

Looking Back

The Wandering Jew

Moby Dick

Ritual Dark Music

New Bigger Ears

Instrumental Albums

Dr Asperger's Klezmer Tonic

Nostalgia's Own End

Rohan Kriwaczek – Funerary Violinist

Salon Concert Music

King David Report -

Two Violins

Circles in the Sand

Live

Rohan Theatre Band albums

Introducing the Infamous Reverend Rohan K.

Love and Loss

Unhealthy Leftovers

Perfect World

Cemetery Songs

Rants and Accusation

Unsavoury Songs

Editor of the Guild of Funerary Violinist's Archive series:

The Art of Funerary Violin

The Funerary Notebooks of Herr Gratchenfleiss

Pierre Dubuisson

Herbert Stanley Littlejohn

Babcotte, Sudbury and Eaton

Find out more at www.rohan-k.co.uk